Praise for L.A. Witt's
Meet Me in the Middle

"Ms. Witt is consistently one of the best m/m authors for me and this book didn't disappoint."

~ *Fiction Vixen*

"A romance that took 20 years to make it but was well worth it in the end. Definitely recommended."

~ *Reviews by Jessewave*

"Witt, along with being the master of angst, is also a master of sexy. Geez! There were times I was sure my Kindle was going to melt."

~ *Joyfully Jay*

"All in all, I loved this story. Way too easy to recommend it for everyone who likes realistic romance, and long-term angst and love."

~ *Top 2 Bottom Reviews*

"At its heart, *Meet Me in the Middle* is a friends-turned-lovers tale, but it's also a story of reunions, friendship, and love lost and found. [...] Be prepared to say 'Aww!' at the end."

~ *Joyfully Reviewed*

Look for these titles by
L.A. Witt

Now Available:

Nine-tenths of the Law
The Distance Between Us
A.J.'s Angel
Out of Focus
The Closer You Get
Conduct Unbecoming
General Misconduct
The Walls of Troy

Tooth & Claw
The Given & the Taken
The Healing & the Dying
The United & the Divided

Writing with Cat Grant
The Only One Who Knows
The Only One Who Matters

Writing with Aleksandr Voinov
No Distance Left to Run

As Lauren Gallagher:

Who's Your Daddy?
All the King's Horses
The Princess and the Porn Star
I'll Show You Mine

Meet Me in the Middle

L.A. Witt

SAMHAIN
PUBLISHING

Samhain Publishing, Ltd.
11821 Mason Montgomery Road, 4B
Cincinnati, OH 45249
www.samhainpublishing.com

Meet Me in the Middle
Copyright © 2013 by L.A. Witt
Print ISBN: 978-1-61921-959-5
Digital ISBN: 978-1-61921-657-0

Editing by Linda Ingmanson
Cover by Lou Harper

First Samhain Publishing, Ltd. electronic publication: August 2013
First Samhain Publishing, Ltd. print publication: August 2014

Dedication

To Aislinn Kerry for telling me what this story was about when I was banging my head against a wall trying to figure it out.

Chapter One

The Mallory-Solomon house was always loaded down with smoking-hot men. Seriously, on any given night, that place was a veritable cornucopia of gorgeous bodies and beautiful faces.

This evening was no exception. Rhett Solomon and his husband, Ethan, were both over the hill, but they sure didn't look the part. Well, okay, Ethan was noticeably gray around the edges, and Rhett had a few lines on his otherwise oh-my-God gorgeous face, but time eventually did that to all of us. Besides, I was pretty sure that living with Ethan or Rhett would've had me aging beyond my years, so I'd say they were doing just fine.

Of course, Kieran Frost was there, sitting on a barstool beside the granite-topped kitchen island where Ethan and Rhett prepared munchies for the evening. In true Wilde's bartender fashion, Kieran was walking eye candy, from his flawless body to his perfectly arranged, almost-black hair. He'd been the much younger plaything that Rhett and Ethan had both been fucking during that dark era a few years back when they'd split up. Apparently, men who fuck hot bartenders together, stay together. Who knew?

Kieran's fiancé was also easy on the eyes. Alex had been naïve and shy when he first met Kieran—a virgin too, from what I'd heard—but Kieran had dragged him out of his shell and duly corrupted him. The kid had even started dressing a little less plainly, opting for some brighter—but still subdued by my standards—colors, things that fit a little tighter and showed a little more skin. The subtle highlights in his dark hair were a nice touch too.

And then there was, of course, yours truly. Like I said, smoking-hot men.

It was movie night in la casa de hot men, which was becoming something of a tradition. Bad movies, obscure movies, mainstream movies; we didn't give a shit as long it was entertaining enough to keep us interested until the second or third bottle of wine kicked in. At that point, anything was interesting. Naturally.

Though odd numbers usually bred odd tension, especially when it was two couples and a single guy, that was never a problem with this group. They were affectionate with each other, but everyone flirted with everyone, so I never felt like a fifth wheel. I'd have stopped showing up a long time ago if I'd been the odd man out.

Sabrina Solomon and her boyfriend had been over to have dinner with her dads earlier in the evening, and shortly after Alex, Kieran and I arrived, the two of them were getting ready to go out.

"Well, look at you." I gestured at Sabrina's absolutely stunning black evening dress. "If I didn't know any better, I'd say a couple of gay men helped you shop."

Rhett rolled his eyes. "You're funny, Dale."

Ethan muttered something and continued slicing cheese for the tray that was already half covered in artfully fanned-out crackers.

Sabrina just giggled. "Actually, it was just one gay guy this time."

"You're welcome." Kieran winked.

"What?" I put a hand to my chest and glared at Kieran. "You never take *me* shopping."

"That's because *you* find shit for *me* to buy, and I end up broke before we stop for dinner."

I shrugged. "Not my fault I have good taste."

"Mm-hmm. Expensive taste is more like it."

Tyson, Sabrina's boyfriend, put an arm around her waist. "Well, at least she's got someone to take her shopping." He smiled, but it was a nervous look, which was odd on someone who was usually so calm and mellow. He seemed in a hurry tonight. Almost twitchy as he said, "Anyway, we'd better run. Doors open at seven."

"Have a good time." Rhett came around the island and kissed Sabrina's cheek. "You know the drill. Call me—"

"If we have too much to drink. I know, Dad." She gave him a pointed look. "Since you're hanging around with these miscreants tonight, are you sure you won't have to call me for the same reason?"

"Very funny."

"Don't worry about it, Mr. Solomon." Tyson shifted his weight from one foot to the other. "We'll just be downtown. We can get a cab if we need to." To Sabrina, he said, "Ready?"

"Yeah, let's go." She hugged both of her dads, said good-bye to the rest of us, and then they headed out of the kitchen with Tyson's hand on the small of her back.

Rhett and Ethan looked toward the hallway until the door had closed. Then they glanced at each other.

"Hundred bucks says he's doing it tonight," Ethan said.

"I don't know." Rhett shook his head. "I was sure he was going to do it last Friday night, and he didn't."

Kieran, Alex and I exchanged puzzled looks.

"What are you two talking about?" Kieran asked. "Is he going to propose or something?"

Rhett nodded. "I'm surprised that ring hasn't burned a hole in his pocket already."

"You know, he actually asked Rhett's permission," Ethan said to us. "I didn't even think people *did* that anymore."

"As if it's my call." Rhett gestured toward the door. "She's the one he needs to ask, not me."

I chuckled. "He was probably just making sure you didn't sic Ethan on him or something."

"Oh, ha, ha." Ethan rolled his eyes.

"He's got a point, actually," Rhett said with a shrug. "You *are* a good deterrent."

"What?" Ethan scoffed.

"Oh, please. You know damn well you're more intimidating than I am." Rhett snatched a piece of cheese off the plate and just barely avoided a swat for his trouble.

Ethan released a huff of breath and turned to Kieran. "See what I put up with? Son of a bitch just uses me to chase off guys who want to date Sabrina."

"Pretty sure that's not the only thing he uses you for," Kieran deadpanned.

"Hmm." Ethan shrugged. "Good point. Fair enough."

Rhett laughed softly, but then he glanced in the direction Sabrina and her boyfriend had gone, and sighed. "God. It was bad enough when she started dating and when she graduated high school. Getting married?" He grimaced and shook his head. "That's...a bit much."

Ethan patted his shoulder. "Welcome to getting old, sweetheart."

"Well," I said, "at least you can find solace in always being younger than Ethan."

Ethan glared at me. Rhett, Alex and Kieran all snickered.

Rhett wrapped his arms around Ethan's waist from behind and kissed his cheek. "He's got a point, you know. That's why I keep you around." Nuzzling Ethan's neck, he added, "You make me feel young."

Ethan elbowed him playfully, and they both laughed.

Alex turned to Kieran. "Hey, aren't you joining that club soon?"

Kieran eyed him. "Which club?"

Flashing him a devilish grin, Alex said, "Why, the club of elderly gay men."

"Oh, shut *up*." Kieran rolled his eyes.

"What?" Ethan arched an eyebrow. "How do *you* get to join? You're not even thirty."

Alex put an arm around Kieran's shoulders and kissed his cheek. "He's just having a bit of a not-quite-midlife crisis."

I laughed. "What the hell? Did you find a gray nipple hair or something?"

"If I did, then it would've meant I was in bed with you."

"Ooh," the other guys said in unison.

"Burn," Alex said.

I flipped Kieran the bird. "You only wish you were in bed with me, darling."

"Keep telling yourself that, Dale." Rhett clapped my shoulder. "So what's the deal, Kieran?"

Alex smirked. "He got an invite to his ten-year high school reunion."

"That's it?" Rhett laughed. "Ethan's coming up on—"

"Zip it." Ethan shot him a glare.

Rhett just laughed again.

"Ugh," Kieran said. "I can't believe it's my ten-year reunion already. Where the hell did a decade go?"

Alex snorted, offering a less than sincere, "Sorry."

Kieran glared at him but then laughed and rolled his eyes again. "You are such a brat, you know that?"

"That's what you get for robbing the cradle," Ethan said. "You get to hear about it every time some little milestone like this comes along."

"You'd know all about that, wouldn't you?" Kieran threw back.

"What? Rhett's not that much younger than me."

"You're still the oldest man in the room, so..."

"Fuck you."

Rhett snickered. "He's got a point, you know. I mean, aren't you coming up on your thirty-year reunion?"

Before Ethan could come back with something snide, Alex broke in. "We're talking about high school reunions, not college."

Ethan's jaw dropped. Rhett, Kieran and I all laughed. Alex wasn't always so forthcoming with the barbs, but when he threw one out there, it was always a good one.

"Well played," Kieran said with a wink.

I rested my elbow on the kitchen island and looked at Kieran. "Well, if it's any consolation, I just got the invite to my *twenty*-year reunion."

"Your twenty-year?" Kieran's eyebrow jumped. "High school?"

I nodded.

He cocked his head. "Did you graduate when you were twenty-five or something?"

"*What?*" I scoffed and stood upright. "Just how old do you think I am?"

He shrugged and gestured at Rhett and Ethan. "Well, you hang around with these senior citizens, so—"

"As do you!"

"Yeah, but you've been part of the group longer. Figured you all evolved out of the Triassic era together."

I exhaled sharply and looked at Rhett. "Why do you guys put up with him again?"

Rhett shrugged. "He gives good head?"

Alex choked on his wine.

"So you claim." I gave Kieran a pointed look. "I have yet to verify this."

Kieran grinned and wrapped his arm around Alex's shoulders. "I have three witnesses. That's enough to convince most juries."

"Well, consider this jury hung," I said.

All four men groaned.

"Oh my God, Dale." Rhett face-palmed. "That was a bad one even for you."

I put up my hands. "What? It's true."

"Mm-hmm." Kieran shook his head.

I just chuckled and took another drink. To this day, I had no idea if Rhett, Ethan and Kieran had curtailed their "extracurricular activities" after Alex came into the picture. Sassy as he was, the kid had been a shy, naïve virgin before Kieran got his hands on him, but I had *complete* faith that Kieran had done his duty and turned Alex into a cock-hungry sex fiend. Whether or not that meant he'd turned their threesomes into foursomes, I didn't know. And if it did, oh Lord, what I wouldn't have given to watch that for a minute or five. Or be in the middle of it.

Before I got carried away with *that* little fantasy again, I shook myself back to life. "And anyway, yes. I'm going to my twenty-year reunion."

Kieran scowled. "You're actually going?"

"Of course. I haven't seen some of these people in years."

"Yeah, I thought that was kind of the idea," Kieran muttered. "If I wanted to stay in touch with them, I would have."

"Well, yes, but there are some I only want to see once every ten or twenty years. You know, see if time was as cruel to the jocks and cheerleaders as the movies always promise it will be." I paused for a sip of wine and then turned more serious. "And I have lost touch with a few people over the years, and this can be a way to reconnect with them. A little more personal than Facebook, you know?"

"Exactly why I'm not going," Kieran said. "I've got some friends from that era, but if I haven't seen them in ten years, I'm not flying to California to get reacquainted with them."

"You never know," I said with a shrug. "Could be fun."

"He's right." Alex nudged Kieran with his elbow. "You could have a good time."

Kieran looked at him. Then he sighed. "Okay. Maybe. I'll think about it."

"Might as well go to this one," Rhett said. "You know, before they start holding your reunions in old folks' homes." He patted Ethan's arm.

"Keep it up," Ethan said, "and you won't have to worry about going to your next reunion."

"You're so adorable when you're menacing." Rhett turned Ethan's chin toward him and kissed him lightly. Ethan tried to glare at him, but they both laughed, and Rhett kissed him again.

Then Ethan looked at us. "So are we going to watch a movie tonight or not?"

Rhett glanced at the clock on the microwave. "We wait too much longer, we're going to fuck up Ethan's bedtime."

"Ass," Ethan muttered. "Come on, let's go see what god-awful DVD Dale brought this time." He paused. "Rhett, would you mind grabbing another bottle of wine?"

"Good idea." Rhett turned to the rest of us. "Anyone else?"

"I'll take a glass," Alex said and downed what was left in his glass.

"Same here," Kieran said. "Can't watch a movie with you guys without some wine."

They all started toward the living room, but I hung back. "You'll probably need an extra pair of hands to carry all that. I'll help."

Rhett glanced at me, but he didn't say anything, and everyone but us cleared out of the kitchen.

As soon as we were alone, I said, "I need a little advice."

"Sure, what's up?" He leaned down to take a bottle off their well-stocked wine rack, but paused. Then he held up a finger and called over his shoulder. "We sticking with red, or does anyone want white?"

There was some murmuring in the other room before Ethan called back, "Red."

"Red it is." Rhett pulled a bottle off the rack. "Sorry about that. What's up?"

I leaned against the kitchen island. "It's about my high school reunion, actually."

"You're going, right?"

"I'm...not sure, to be honest."

"Oh?" Rhett looked up from opening the bottle. "What's wrong?"

"Well, there's a lot of people I want to see, but..." I exhaled. "Let's put it this way. If I could see a list of who else is coming before I committed and bought my ticket, that would help me make the decision."

"Someone in particular you want to see?"

"Someone in particular I *don't* want to see."

"*Ooh.*" He set the cork and corkscrew on the counter. "An ex?"

"Well, he's not an ex, per se," I said. "We never dated. We just...fucked. Once after graduation, and again at our last reunion."

Rhett's eyebrows rose. "I could see how that might make this reunion awkward."

"You think?"

Brow furrowed as he thought for a moment, Rhett idly thumbed his wedding ring. "Mind if I ask something personal?"

I picked up the bottle of wine to start pouring the glasses. "Shoot."

He hesitated. Then, "What would you do if you saw him again?"

I set the bottle down. The question hammered itself into my consciousness. Right into my bones. What *would* I do? I shook my head slowly. "I don't know. I mean, it's been ten years, but it's..."

"Still raw?"

"For lack of a better word, yes."

Rhett took the bottle back, and as he poured, said, "What exactly happened? I mean, obviously you slept together, but"—he gave me one of his patented "looks"—"you've fucked plenty of guys and never batted an eye. Something else must have happened."

I watched the wine accumulating in each glass in turn, because that meant not acknowledging Rhett's scrutiny. "It was...complicated."

"Isn't it always?"

"Sex? No." I grinned. "Sex can be very, very simple." My grin fell. I reached for one of the glasses he'd already poured, and swallowed most of the wine in a single go.

Rhett blinked. "Must have been really complicated." He took my glass back and refilled it. "What happened?"

I exhaled. "Friendship gone sour after a couple of fucks that probably shouldn't have happened."

"Ouch."

"Tell me about it."

"Will there be people at the reunion you *do* want to see?"

"Probably, yeah."

"Then go." He set the bottle aside and looked at me. "Don't let this guy control you and keep you from people you want to spend time with."

"And if he's there?"

Rhett waved a hand. "Don't worry about him. It's been ten years. You deserve to be able to go to this thing, see people from your past, and have a good time."

I focused on the granite countertop between us. That was the logical solution, of course. "A little easier said than done, don't you think?"

"Ooh, yeah." When I looked at him, Rhett grimaced. "You may recall I've got some experience with being in the same building with someone I didn't want to see."

"Very true." I was fairly certain the entire damned city remembered when he and Ethan were stuck living in the same house after they'd split up. The silver lining was that it had ultimately brought Kieran into our social circle, but the two-year downward spiral and the short period between breaking up and making up? Jesus. I thought they'd kill each other.

"Honestly?" I said. "Part of me wants to see him."

Rhett's eyebrows rose. "Which part?"

"Not *that* one." I laughed, but it didn't last. "I don't know, I guess I feel like I need some closure after the way things went down before. It's been bugging me all this time, and I can't decide if seeing him again will just make it worse, or if it'll give me a chance to put it to rest."

Right then, Ethan appeared in the doorway, his lips curled into their customary smirk. "You guys letting the wine age or something?"

From behind him, Kieran called out, "Ethan doesn't have time to wait for it to—"

"That's enough out of you," Ethan threw over his shoulder. He rolled his eyes and looked at us again. His smirk faded. "Everything okay in here?"

Rhett looked at me.

I smiled and picked up three of the wineglasses. "Everything's fine."

Ethan eyed me skeptically. "You sure?"

"Don't worry about it," Rhett said. They exchanged one of those long, loaded looks they'd perfected after almost a decade and a half together, and Ethan nodded like he'd received whatever message Rhett had been conveying. Then he disappeared back into the living room, and Rhett turned to me again. "You still have feelings for this guy?"

"I'm... Oh hell, I'm not even sure. I mean, we were close friends all through high school, and then we fucked at our graduation party, and then we didn't speak until our ten-year reunion." I released an exasperated sigh. "And then we fucked again and haven't spoken since." Pausing, I shook my head. "And it's not even that simple. There's...more to it. But..."

Rhett watched me silently for a long moment. "Can I offer one piece of unsolicited advice?"

"Rhett, darling, I pulled you aside to talk to you. Any advice is hardly unsolicited."

He half shrugged. "Okay, point taken. But, listen. Whatever happened, you obviously have some lingering hang-ups about this guy."

"So, you don't think I should go to the reunion?"

"No, I think you should go. Just promise me you won't fuck this guy if he's there."

I snorted. "Sweetheart, please. After the last two times? Anything he tries to put in me is getting cut off and handed back to him on a platter."

Rhett threw his head back and laughed. "Ever the eloquent one, Dale."

"And that's why you love me."

"I wouldn't go quite that far. Now grab those wineglasses and let's go see if this DVD is any good."

Chapter Two

For about three weeks, I hemmed and hawed about going to the reunion. Finally, I gave in and bought a ticket. Then a plane ticket. *Orlando, darling, here I come.*

I took a couple of extra days off work so I could visit family while I was in town, but before I knew it, Friday night had arrived. Showtime. After a lengthy pep talk in my hotel room mirror, and another in the rental car's rearview, I headed out.

The reunion committee had been busy. They'd snagged the ballroom at a hotel on the beach, which was usually booked solid ages in advance. It was just a block down the road from the place where we'd had our senior party. That restaurant and pool hall had long since been sold, renovated and reopened as a seafood place I'd never heard of, but just driving past it was enough to wake up some dormant butterflies in my stomach. I could still taste the ashes of the clandestine cigarettes we'd sneaked away from the party. I hadn't touched a cigarette in fifteen years, hadn't touched *him* in ten, but all it took was a drive past that familiar squat little building beneath the row of swaying palm trees to take me back.

So what would happen if we were in the same room tonight?

Nothing, I informed myself. That was what would happen. Not a goddamned thing, because twenty years had passed since the first time and ten since the last, and I had moved on. Some closure would have been nice, but it wasn't like those nights kept me awake anymore. Well, aside from last night. And a few nights before I flew down here.

But generally speaking, the only time it bothered me was when I stopped and thought about it. It was one of those things everyone had, those memories they looked back on and wondered what it would've been like if things had worked out differently. In fact, I hadn't even thought about it in a good long time before the invite to the reunion showed up in my e-mail box. It was less of a thorn in my side as it was a small grain of sand in my shoe. I didn't always feel it, but when I did, it was irritating as hell.

If he was here tonight, then so be it. We could be cordial. We were adults. Everything that had ever happened between us was far enough behind me now. And even if I still had the occasional sand-in-my-shoe feeling about those two nights, odds were he'd moved on.

For that matter, he'd aged a fair amount from graduation to our ten-year reunion. Ten more years had probably eroded away all the features that had attracted me to him in the first place. I doubted he was anywhere near the silver fox Ethan was.

Silver fox? For Christ's sake, he was *my* age. Ugh. I was not getting old. Certainly not old enough to be a silver anything, fox or otherwise.

I was not getting old, but hopefully he was. And not very gracefully. If he'd managed to avoid getting kicked out of the navy, he was probably still in shape, so the least he could do was go bald, damn it. He owed me that much.

I parked and walked into the hotel. The line at the door was long, full of familiar faces I'd all but forgotten about.

Our class had evolved just like most classes did. The jocks got fat, the nerds got rich, and the stoners wound up with MBAs and BMWs. Craig Wilson's baseball-star days were far behind him, and I'd heard he still lived at home with his parents, his ego and his growing beer gut. Nicki Foster was still waiting on tables and wishing on stars in Hollywood, while Jess

Brown had given up on Broadway in favor of a family and a management position at some hippie organic free-range grocer in New York.

I'd heard through the grapevine that Ryan Gartner, voted Nerdiest of all the Nerds back in the day, had made a fortune in some field involving microchips. The microchip part could have been bullshit, but the fortune part must have been true, because from where I was standing, it looked like he had a Swiss watch on one arm and a Swiss supermodel on the other. Well done, Gartner. Well done.

And there was something poetic and more than a little gratifying about seeing Steve Hiatt the homophobic bully traipsing in through the door with highlighted hair, shoes I would have sold my soul to own, and a boyfriend who *had* to be a cover model for romance novels.

For every face I did see, there were at least a dozen I didn't. Maybe they hadn't arrived, or maybe they weren't coming at all. One in particular was noticeably absent, but I tried not to think about him. Which was easy, of course. Well, except when I heard a male voice that vaguely resembled his. Or caught a glimpse of someone with similarly broad shoulders. Or that military-cut dark hair.

I took a deep breath and steeled myself. If he was here tonight, I'd deal with it. One way or another, though, I was having a good time.

I made it to the front of the line, handed over my ticket— *nope, just me; no plus one, no date, no husband or boyfriend or totally just-for-shock-value wife*—and went into the ballroom.

As soon as I stepped through the door, the open bar grabbed my attention. Now that was a damned good start. After a short wait in line and a little flirting with the *cute* bartender, I scored a dry martini and then casually made my way toward the growing crowd in search of pleasantly familiar faces.

"Dale?" A female voice spun me around. "Dale Ramsey? Is that you?"

It took a second for her face to click in my memory, but then I held out my arms. "Jennifer! My God, it's good to see you."

"I thought that was you." She threw her arms around me. "How have you been, sweetheart? Are you still up in Seattle?"

I returned her embrace, and as I pulled back, I said, "Yep, still living in the rainy city. What are you up to these days, darling?"

"Staying at home and raising kids," she said.

"Oh yeah? How many?"

"Three." She smiled. "Do you want to see pictures?"

"Woman, of course I want to see pictures." I snapped my fingers a few times. "Whip 'em out. Come on."

She laughed and pulled her phone out of her purse. After a second or two of scrolling, she turned the screen toward me, revealing a photo of three young children. "Madison is six, Troy is almost four, and Christopher is five months."

"Five months?" I stepped back and looked her up and down. "You had a baby five months ago?"

Jennifer nodded. "Still losing some of the weight, but I'm almost—"

"Oh, darling, you look spectacular," I said. "And knowing you just had a baby? Jesus fuck, my dear, I know a few people who'd cut off limbs for your secret."

"The secret?" She snorted. "It's called 'keeping up with two little ones and an infant'."

"Hmm. I'll stick to the gym."

She laughed. "So what about you? Do you have a boyfriend or something these days?"

I shook my head. "Nope, 'fraid not."

25

"Dale." She huffed. "You're really letting me down here."

"What?" I eyed her. "Honey, I'm the one who's not getting any, not you."

"Yeah, but what good is a gay friend if he doesn't bring his hot boyfriends around for us bored housewives to ogle?"

"I guess you'll just have to settle for me, *mi amore.*" I closed my eyes and stretched my arms out to the sides. "All right. I'm ready. Ogle me."

Another female voice came from beside me: "Ooh, ten minutes in, and Dale's already soaking up the spotlight."

I opened my eyes and grinned when I saw another old friend. "Kelly! Sweetheart! Get over here and give me a hug!"

She hugged me, and the three of us caught up for a few minutes. Jobs, families, hushed whispers of "Did you *hear* what happened to so-and-so?"—the usual class-reunion conversation.

Then Jennifer leaned in close to Kelly, lifting a finger off her wineglass to point at something across the room. "Is that who I think it is?"

Kelly furrowed her brow and looked past me. "Holy crap. Yeah, that's definitely him."

"Definitely who?" I turned around.

I should have known. I should have fucking known.

Oh, my Lord, but time was good to him.

Adam O'Connor. You sexy son of a bitch.

He wasn't looking my way, thank God, which gave me a moment to quietly drink him in while I also drank the last of this martini in one go. I didn't have to ask if he was still in the navy. The haircut, the posture; yeah, he was still a sailor. He had more gray than I expected, though. Most of his hair was black, but his temples and the very edges of his hairline were getting lighter. I might have thought that served him right, except he even wore gray hair well. Jerk. Time had added a few lines, weathering him like it weathered all of us, but he was definitely abusing the privilege of being a fine wine. One that didn't look like it'd be turning to vinegar anytime soon.

Adam turned his head, and I didn't have a chance to pretend I was looking elsewhere before our eyes met.

He excused himself from his conversation and headed toward me. My heart went into my throat. The martini I'd just finished was suddenly nowhere near strong enough.

And the next thing I knew, he was right there. Right in front of me. Beer in hand, eyes locked on mine, that reserved smile curling up the corners of his lips, there he was.

"Dale," he said. "It's good to see you."

I smiled in spite of my racing heart. "You too. I didn't think you'd be here."

Adam chuckled. "Well, I almost didn't make it. Wasn't sure I'd get my leave approved, but here I am."

Yes, here you are.

He muffled a cough. "So, are you here with anyone?"

"No," I said. "You?"

Avoiding my eyes, Adam shook his head. "Nope. Just me."

"So you and—" I glanced at his left hand. The third finger was bare without so much as a tan line. "Oh."

"Things didn't work out," he said.

"Sorry to hear it."

Beside me, Kelly cleared her throat. "Hey, we're going to go refill our drinks. We'll catch up with you guys, though, okay?"

"Okay." *Don't abandon me. Not now. Please stay...*

But she looped her arm through Jennifer's elbow, and the two of them disappeared into the thickening crowd, leaving me with...him.

I shifted my weight. "So, you're still in the navy, then?"

He nodded. "Retiring in a few months, though."

"Retiring before fifty?" I managed a smile. "Must be nice."

"One of the perks of the job."

"What will you do next?"

"Don't know yet. I'm still working that part out." He paused. "So what are you doing these days?"

Funny how everyone asked that question at a reunion, but coming from him, it threw me off. *Why do you care? Why are we having this conversation?*

I cleared my throat. "Same as ever. Still living in Seattle, still working at the same place as before."

We made more mundane conversation, catching up on the very superficial basics, but I barely heard a word either of us said. I knew seeing him again would be jarring, and I'd been dreading it, but I hadn't expected it to hurt like this. That deep ache in my chest was a shock. Emotions that I'd thought were long dead started clawing their way to the surface. How much I'd secretly wanted him when I still thought he was straight, but kept it to myself rather than make things awkward with my best friend since grade school. How hard I'd fallen for him even when I'd known he'd be gone too soon to make anything work. And how hard I'd fallen again—fallen for him, fallen on my face—ten years later. That grain of sand in my shoe had somehow grown into a red-hot ember of regret.

I'd figured I might be angry when I saw him, or that I might be tempted to toss a drink in his face, and I was right on both counts, but that fury came from all the other emotions. What right did he have to still have such a hold on me?

The conversation hit a natural lull, and I seized the opportunity. "Well, I think I'm going to go get some air. It was, um, nice seeing you again."

"Yeah, you too."

I was tempted to stop by the bar for another—and much stronger—martini, but the need for some fresh air won me over, so I walked out onto the patio behind the ballroom. I leaned against the railing and took a deep breath of the cool, salty air. Big mistake. The beach smelled just like it had after our graduation party, and one taste of that wind sent me right back to that night.

"Can you believe they won't let us have cigarettes?" Adam flipped the ink-black fringe out of his eyes. "We're adults. We're not in high school anymore. We should be allowed to fucking smoke."

"Yeah, but after tonight, just let them try and stop us."

He grinned, that grin that always made me wish he wasn't straight and we could share more than just cigarettes. "You're right." And then his eyes narrowed a little in true devilish Adam form. "Want to sneak out for one? For old time's sake?"

If it means a little more time with you, then... "Hell yeah."

We worked our way through the crowd of classmates and slipped out the back. From there, we wandered down the steps and through the shadows until the hard ground became soft sand. There were no chairs out here, but a knee-high piece of driftwood made as good a bench as anything.

I pulled a wrinkled pack of smokes out of my back pocket.

"Good thing one of us came prepared," Adam said.

"I'm always prepared."

For anything. Which was why I also had a couple of condoms and some lube with me. I'd had my eye on a couple of guys in our class, and at least one had had his eye on me too.

29

With some luck and a little finesse, I was going to fuck the hell out of him before this night was over.

But first, a cigarette with my best friend. The last time we'd ever have to sneak off for a smoke.

We each pulled a cigarette from the pack, lit them, and then I set the pack and lighter between us on the driftwood.

"Remember when we cut out of Mrs. Harrison's class?" Adam tapped some ashes over the sand in front of our feet. "The time your dad almost caught us?"

I laughed. "Why do you think I was so scared to cut class after that?" I shook my head. "I'd rather sit through one of Mrs. Harrison's lectures than face my dad with an infraction."

"I don't know. I'd have to sit down and think about that one."

"Because you wouldn't have had to face my dad."

"Precisely." He took another drag. "So when did you say you were leaving for Washington?"

"Middle of August." I slowly dug a deep groove in the sand with the toe of my shoe. "Man, it's going to be weird living in Seattle."

"Yeah. I hear it's fucking cold. And all that rain."

"I'll manage," I said. "I just can't believe *you're* leaving so soon."

Adam sighed, blowing out a long stream of smoke into the night air. Then he flicked his spent cigarette into the sand. "I was kinda hoping for one last summer, but...I don't know. Figured it would be better to just get it over with." He laughed softly. "Didn't want to be stuck in boot camp over the winter. Not when it's in fucking Illinois."

"Yeah, I guess you wouldn't," I said with a halfhearted laugh. "And you're in for four years?"

Adam nodded.

"We'll both be done around the same time, then." I glanced at him, managing a slight smile. "You'll be getting out, and I'll be graduating."

"Yeah." He looked out at the ocean. "It depends, though. I might stay longer. If I like it, I mean."

"Oh. Wow." So weird, the prospect of leaving our hometown and going our separate ways. Especially for so long. Maybe forever. I took the last little bit of smoke from my cigarette and exhaled it slowly as I tossed the butt in the sand. "I'm not gonna lie. I'm gonna miss you."

"I'm gonna miss you too." Adam brushed some hair out of his face and looked in my eyes. "But I'm not gone yet."

My heart beat faster. When Adam slid a little closer, the cigarette pack crinkling against him, I pulled in a breath, one that tasted like smoke and the ocean air.

"I know I leave pretty soon," he said, almost whispering. "But, we do have tonight."

I gulped. "W-we do?"

"Yeah." God, he was even closer now. "We do."

Though I was still trying to figure out what the hell was happening, I couldn't help leaning toward him. And every tiny move we made, everything I felt, seemed to make a kiss inevitable, but what the hell did I know? Especially since Adam was *straight*.

He reached for my face. Hesitated. Drew his hand back a little.

My heart pounded even harder. I moistened my lips, and he jumped. Then he reached for me again, and this time he came all the way across the divide and touched my cheek. His fingertips were warm and unsteady. As he leaned closer, the cigarette wrapper crinkled again. The lighter clattered off the side of the driftwood and landed dully on the sand.

The tip of his nose brushed mine.

"Dale..." He closed some more of the distance. I thought he might say something, finish whatever thought he'd started. I couldn't imagine how he could think any better than I could. Our lips were so close together, not quite there but way past the point we could pretend we weren't heading toward a kiss.

Behind us, our classmates laughed and carried on with Boyz II Men playing in the background. In front of us, the tide lazily rolled out. But everything immediately around us was completely still and silent. We hovered on either side of a thinning line between backing off and going through with this, lips almost touching. Adam's thumb drew a gentle arc across my cheekbone, and I sucked in a breath at his soft touch.

"God, Dale," he breathed, and crossed that line. His kiss wasn't nearly as hesitant as the moment leading up to it. He pressed his lips to mine like he meant it, and he kissed me hard enough to bring every fantasy I'd ever had about him right to the forefront of my mind.

He drew back. His dark eyes were barely visible in the low light, but I could see him.

Adam. I couldn't comprehend that *Adam* had kissed me. My lips were still tingling with a smoke-flavored kiss, and the man facing me was the one who'd kissed me, and that man was definitely Adam, his distinctive unruly fringe fluttering in the breeze, but I couldn't pull those pieces together. It didn't make sense. How?

But there was no way around it either. Adam had kissed me. Really kissed me like there was no reason he shouldn't have.

I stared at him, forcing my eyes to focus in the darkness so I could be sure this was really him and not some body double. Not some trick or prank or out-of-control fantasy.

When I finally spoke, I sputtered, "You're...*gay*?"

Adam didn't speak. He pulled me in for another kiss, and, well, that answered that. I wrapped my arms around him and shivered as his hand slid from my side to the middle of my back. The cigarette pack crinkled between us, pressed between his leg and mine. I tilted my head and parted my lips, opening up to as much as he was willing to give, and shivered again as the tip of his tongue slid under mine.

"Why the hell did we never do this before?" he whispered.

"You tell me." I was shaking so much, all nerves and arousal and *tell me this is real.*

"Do you—" He paused, swallowing hard. "Do you want to go somewhere else?"

"No. I want to stay right here."

I kissed him again, and he kissed me back, and while our classmates partied away our last few hours between high school and the real world, Adam and I held on for the rest of the night.

"They couldn't have picked a better night for this."

Adam's voice startled me back into the present.

I gritted my teeth. Apparently he hadn't realized that *"I'm going to get some air"* meant *"I need to be away from you so I can put myself back together."* Fair enough, I supposed. What kind of idiot let himself be thrown off like this after a five-minute conversation with a friend he'd fucked a couple of times in another lifetime?

Stupid as it might have been, I couldn't make myself look at him. Replaying that long-dormant memory had opened up some wounds I wasn't ready to deal with, and my death grip on the wooden railing was all that stood between me and creating some new wounds on that son of a bitch's face.

Oblivious to the emotions charging through me, Adam put his hands on the railing and leaned over them. Looking out at the ocean, he took a deep breath in through his nose. "Man, that takes me back."

It sure does, I didn't say.

"Almost makes me wish I hadn't quit smoking," he said.

I stiffened. "Oh really?" A second too late, I realized I'd opened the door for us to discuss That Night, so I quickly said, "When did you quit?"

"About five years ago." He looked at me—I didn't look at him, but I could see him with my peripheral vision—and asked, "You still smoke?"

I gritted my teeth again. "I stopped smoking before the last reunion." This time, I did turn toward him, narrowing my eyes as I said, "Or don't you remember?"

Adam's eyes widened. He drew back a little. "I...well... Dale, it's been a long time. I don't remember everything."

Exhaling, I reached up to rub the back of my neck. Maybe I wasn't being fair. I'd probably forgotten a lot of things about him too. We were measuring the space between visits in decades.

"Sorry. I..." I shook my head. Nothing I could have said would've made that moment any less awkward, so I just repeated, "Sorry."

He was quiet for a moment. Then, "Listen, about last time. We—"

"It was ten years ago," I snapped. "Let's just let it go."

He glared out at the ocean.

I pulled in a breath and squared my shoulders. "Look, I came all the way here to catch up with friends, not rehash whatever it was we did. If you'll excuse me, I'd like to get my money's worth."

Calling on every bit of self-control I had left, I turned to go.

Adam stopped me with a hand on my arm. "Dale. Wait."

I didn't turn around.

"It was a long time ago," he said quietly. "I—"

"Yes, it was a long time ago." I closed my eyes, cursing the emotions tightening my throat. "And the fact that it still hurts after all this time should tell you something."

"It does."

I turned. "What?"

He released my arm. "I'm not asking you to forget it. All that time that's gone by since then, it gave me a lot of time to think about things. And realize I'd made a mistake. A lot of them, actually."

I swallowed, uncertain what to say.

"We were friends once too," he said. "Remember?"

"Of *course* I remember," I said through my teeth, the words barely coming out as a whisper.

He held my gaze for a long moment, and I knew that look. He had something he wanted to say; he just wasn't sure how to say it.

I set my jaw. "Out with it. Whatever it is."

He looked away, focusing out on the dark void of the ocean.

"Adam."

He took a deep breath. "I know you came all this way to see people and get caught up, not sort out old issues. And I don't want to keep you from anyone." He gestured at the ballroom where our old friends talked and drank. "Go catch up. But, could I talk you into meeting me for coffee tomorrow?"

I chewed my lip. That was a bad idea. A seriously bad idea.

But we had had a friendship at one time or another, a friendship I'd dearly missed after we'd parted ways, and maybe we could salvage that if nothing else. Or bury the hatchet and part ways with some actual closure.

"Okay. Text me tomorrow and we'll...we'll figure something out."

We exchanged phone numbers. Then I went back inside while Adam hung back on the patio. He came in a while later, and I saw him a few times while we both caught up with people, but we stayed apart for the rest of the evening. A few exchanged glances, some longer than others, but no crossing paths. No speaking. No interacting.

Which only made me that much more nervous about tomorrow.

Chapter Three

When/where do you want to meet up?

I glared at my phone and thought, *How about the twelfth of never?*

But I couldn't deny I did want to see him again. Maybe we could settle this and finally move on, since apparently that grain of sand in my shoe was bigger than I thought.

I looked out the window. Across the street was a small coffee shop that didn't look too crowded and hopefully wouldn't give us food poisoning. Looked like the kind of hipster place that poured coffee that wouldn't offend my Seattle-coffee-snob palate. I texted Adam the name and address, along with a suggestion of meeting in an hour and a half or so, and then tossed my phone on the bed. Time to grab a shower, get dressed and put myself together for a casual cup of coffee, *not* a date.

As I walked outside an hour or so later, I swore under my breath. When I'd texted him, I'd chosen the location that required the least amount of travel and inconvenience on my part. Petty? Passive aggressive? Yeah, just a little. I was a vindictive bitch, what could I say?

But there was one detail I hadn't taken into consideration: I'd picked the coffee shop right across the street from my goddamned hotel. Convenient as fuck if I wanted to drag someone back to my room and—

No. Fuck no. Not this time. I was not sleeping with him. No way. Fool me once, fool me twice and all that crap. He wasn't fooling me a third time.

We'd have coffee, and we'd bury the hatchet. If he played his cards right, I might even bury that hatchet somewhere other than in his skull.

Sighing, I ran a hand through my hair. I wasn't being fair at all. Yeah, the past hurt, but it was the past. The *distant* past. If I was angry at anything, it was my inability to let go of the hurt after all this time.

I ordered a coffee and took a seat at one of the tables outside.

Three sips into my cappuccino, I decided I should've ordered decaf. Sacrilege, of course, but I was too jittery to add any caffeine to the mix.

This was ridiculous. I was an idiot for being so damned nervous. But then, this conversation was a decade or two overdue, so I supposed a few butterflies were warranted. The fact that I was saturating those butterflies in caffeine was my own fault.

I glanced at my phone. Still another fifteen minutes before he'd be along, assuming he was still as insanely punctual as he'd always been. I wrapped my hands around my coffee cup, seeking warmth to ward off a phantom chill in spite of the Florida heat.

Was I even justified in being bitter? We'd both known after graduation that he'd be leaving for boot camp in under a month. At our last reunion, I'd known damn well he was separated from his wife. Even if she didn't suddenly decide to reconcile with him, I would have been his rebound.

He'd never deliberately hurt me, at least not as far as I could tell. I couldn't justify being angry at him for anything malicious. But the fact remained, I had been hurt. By the loss of our friendship, and by his sudden about-face about pursuing something with me. Victim of circumstance, maybe, but it still hurt, and Adam had never been terribly forthcoming with anything beyond a cursory apology. One that had a habit of coming about ten years later than it should have.

Right on time, Adam came around the corner. I took and released a long breath as I watched him come up the sidewalk. He was dressed down today, trading last night's polo shirt and slacks for a pair of khaki shorts and a plain T-shirt. Sandals too, but at least he'd had the decency to not wear socks with them.

Because he's not from Seattle. Duh.

He stopped beside my table and cleared his throat. "Hey."

"Hi." I rested my elbows on the table and clasped my fingers loosely together. "So, you wanted to talk."

"Yeah." He nodded toward the coffee shop. "I'm just going to, um..."

"Right. I'll be here."

"Okay."

As he disappeared into the coffee shop, I released my breath. We could do this. It was just coffee and a conversation. Salvage a friendship, or at least make peace and move on.

I noped.

A few minutes later, the other chair scraped on the concrete, and I looked up as Adam took a seat.

"So." He tapped his fingers on both sides of his coffee cup. "This... um..."

"So you're single now."

Adam flinched. He slid his right hand over his left, but not fast enough to keep me from confirming that both his ring and tan line were gone. "I've been single for a while."

"Yeah?" I picked up my coffee. "Define a while. And single, as long as we're on the subject." Well, wasn't this off to a charming start? *Settle down, Dale. Jesus.* I hadn't intended all that bitterness to come bubbling up to the surface in the form of a swipe like that, but... Hell, I didn't know what I thought or expected or anything about this conversation. So much for being over it.

Adam sat back. He rested his hands in his lap and sighed as he cocked his head like he often did when he was exasperated. "Dale."

"Don't look at me like that, Adam." Damn my voice for shaking. "I think it's a legitimate question, don't you?"

He lowered his gaze. For a moment, he was quiet. Then, speaking softly, he said, "Jackie and I split up for good about a year after I went back to her."

"Oh." I didn't know how to feel about that. Maybe I'd felt vindictive and catty a minute ago, but even a decade's worth of bitterness wasn't enough for me to feel smug or triumphant over the fact that their marriage, the one he'd gone back to instead of continuing with me, had ultimately failed. It was bad enough I'd gotten hurt in this. His ex-wife didn't deserve it. And in spite of my bitterness, I couldn't really even convince myself he did.

I blew out a breath. "Okay, maybe we're getting off on the wrong foot here. And I'm...sorry. I didn't mean for..." What did I mean? Fuck if I knew.

"It's okay," he said quietly. He leaned forward again and folded his arms on the table. "Look, we need to clear the air about the past."

"We do." I paused. "Which means I need you to be honest with me about something. Just...so I can have a little peace of mind."

Adam nodded. "Yeah, sure."

I moistened my lips. "When we hooked up at the last reunion, were you two..." I couldn't even bring myself to form the words.

He took a deep breath but didn't look at me. "We were separated."

"*How* separated?"

Adam met my eyes and furrowed his brow. "What do you mean?"

"Getting counseling? Working on it? Not speaking?" I inclined my head. "Were you guys really heading toward a divorce, or trying to get back on track?"

Lowering his gaze, he didn't speak. Seconds ground past, and my heart sank deeper. His lingering silence spoke volumes.

I forced back the ache in my throat and wished I'd never even asked. I should've known by then not to ask questions unless I was sure I wanted the answers. "That's all I really wanted to know." I started to get up.

"Wait," Adam said.

I stopped.

"Look," he said. "It was a complicated situation. She'd left me, and yeah, we'd been talking, but by the time I came to the reunion, I thought it was over. That there was no chance. And I was trying to move on."

I eased myself back into my chair. Not because I wanted to stay, but because I wasn't so sure I could rely on my legs. "But if the door had been open..."

Adam sighed, lowering his gaze again.

"And if you had known that night that she'd suggest getting back together," I said, barely forcing a whisper past my lips, "would we...?"

A long moment passed before he shook his head. "No. No, we wouldn't have." He exhaled. "I didn't go into it to use you, I just... Look, I didn't know she and I were going to get back together, and—"

"Then what was it you wanted from me?" I asked. "Just sex? Or did you think there might be something else right up until the point your wife decided to give you another chance?"

"I had no idea what I wanted then." The unsteadiness in his voice gave me pause. "For God's sake, Dale, do you think I just wanted to use you?"

"I don't know if that's what you wanted or not," I said. "But it's what you did. *Twice.*"

"That's not true," he threw back. "We both knew the first time that I was leaving."

"But I didn't think you were walking out of my life completely." I ground my teeth. "You still had three weeks from the time we graduated until the time you left for boot camp, and I saw you, what, twice? And I wrote to you. In boot camp."

He didn't look at me. "I know."

"Then why didn't you ever write back?"

"Because I didn't..." He rubbed his forehead with this thumb and forefinger, then took a deep breath and lowered his hand. "I didn't know what to say."

"You didn't have a lot of trouble smooth-talking me at the last reunion."

He scowled. "I guess I didn't realize that night how long you can hold a grudge."

"And I didn't realize that night how fucking disposable I was to you."

"Dale, she was my wife!"

"And what the fuck was I?" I shook my head. "I never would have asked you to choose between her and me. You married her. You obviously loved her. I respect that. But I can't just be the hole you put your dick in when the one you really want decides she's through with you."

He flinched. "That was never what you were, and you know it."

"Do I?" I narrowed my eyes. "Then explain to me how we were like this"—I held up two crossed fingers—"right up until the night we fucked for the first time?"

Adam's lips parted. "I..."

"I could have dealt with us fucking and then moving on," I said, loathing the way my voice cracked. "But we were friends before that. What happened to that?"

Adam lowered his gaze. "I'm sorry. There's really nothing more I can say."

"I suppose there isn't." I took a deep breath and hoped I could at least keep the tears back if I couldn't keep my voice steady. "Listen, I'm not your toy or anyone else's. I'm not your spare to keep around for—"

"I've never used you like that, Dale. I know it hurt when I left. And I'm sorry. I...I didn't know how to process all of this the first time, and I had no idea Jackie and I would try to patch things up after the second time."

"What do you think would have happened if she hadn't?" I clenched my teeth, not sure if I really wanted the answer to that.

"What good is speculating about it?" he asked. "I went back to her. Things didn't work out with her. They didn't work out with you." He half shrugged, his shoulder rising almost imperceptibly as if he'd had the weight of the world resting on it. "What's the point of torturing ourselves with 'what if'?"

"Maybe a little peace of mind," I said. "Knowing I actually meant something to you."

His spine straightened. "Of course you meant something to me, Dale. You know that."

"Do I?"

He just stared at me, eyes wide.

I shifted in my chair. "You know, after our senior party? It was almost two years before I slept with anyone again. I had plenty of opportunity in college, believe me, but I just couldn't do it. *That* is how much that night meant to me, and how much it fucked with me when you just disappeared off the radar."

Adam's lips parted. "Was it... That wasn't your first time, though, was it?"

"No." I sniffed sharply. "It was my first time with you."

He stared at me. "Dale..."

I swallowed. I'd promised myself I wouldn't let my emotions get the best of me today, and I was doing a bang-up job of that.

He reached for my arm but withdrew his hand when I pulled my arm back. "I never knew it meant that much to you."

You *meant that much to me, you son of a bitch.*

Neither of us said anything. I wasn't sure what there was to say. There was a time when we didn't just finish each other's sentences, we started them. We knew each other that well. But that was a long time ago. The man sitting across from me wasn't even a man who'd left me twisting in the wind. He was a stranger. A complete and total stranger.

And maybe that was why I'd agreed to meet him for coffee, to confirm what I already knew. Adam and I had both moved on. Maybe there were lingering feelings and resentment, but we had become different people. What existed between us before was gone now.

I cleared my throat. "Look, we both know friendships come and go. And how many really live past high school, right?"

Without looking at me, Adam nodded.

"Maybe ours was just meant to end there," I said.

"Maybe it was."

He still didn't meet my eyes, and looking at him only made it harder for me to compose myself enough to call time on this conversation.

I took a deep breath. "I'm going to go." I gathered up my coffee cup and napkin and stood. "It was, um, good seeing you."

"Yeah." His eyes flicked up. "You too."

We held each other's gazes for a moment, something unspoken pulsing in the taut air between us, but I turned to leave before either of us could break that tense silence. He didn't stop me. I threw away my coffee cup, waited for a break in traffic and crossed over to my hotel, and Adam didn't move. On the way into the lobby, I stole a glance at him in the tinted glass door, and his back was still to me, his head bowed a little like he was rubbing his eyes or something. I didn't even know if that was insulting or a relief, the fact that he didn't even watch me go.

Doesn't matter. Just go.

As soon as I was through the front door, I released my breath. I stopped for a moment just to collect myself and catch my breath. My heart was pounding like I'd just run ten blocks instead of strolling across the street, and my knees were a little unsteady.

Seeing him still hurt too much for me to say I'd found closure, but at least I knew where I stood with him. The closure would come once I went home and moved on, once I could think about him without this ache in my chest. No, when I didn't think of him at all.

Right now, though, it definitely hurt. Walking away was almost as painful as sitting there with him, but what choice did I have? The fact was, I wanted him, but not as badly as I didn't want to have him and then lose him again.

I continued through the lobby and stopped in front of the elevator. I stabbed the Up button with my thumb.

"Dale, wait."

Fuck. *Really?* I cringed, then turned around as Adam sprinted across the lobby.

"What?" I growled. "Was I supposed to pay for your coffee too?"

"No." He stopped beside me. "There's just a little more I need to say before I go."

The elevator dinged, and the doors opened. Adam's eyebrows knitted together, an unspoken plea for me to just hear him out. After a moment, the doors closed. He glanced at them, then at me, eyebrows up again.

"Fine," I said. "Just say what you need to say and be done with it, all right?"

He set his shoulders back. "Listen, I should have been honest with you about Jackie, and I should have stayed in touch when I left for the navy, but I need you to know that you were never just someone to fuck because my wife had kicked me out. You were never just a convenient fuck."

"So you've said. Then what was I?"

"You were..." He took a deep breath. Released it. Looked at the floor between us. "You..."

"Forget I asked." I stabbed the elevator button again.

The doors started to open, and Adam grabbed my arm. "I don't know what to call you, Dale," he said, speaking quickly. "You were always just you. Just...just Dale."

"Oh." I wrenched my arm away. "I'm fucking touched." I stepped into the elevator.

The doors started closing, and he stopped it with his hand and stepped in with me. Before I could tell him to get the fuck out, he said, "I don't think you understand."

"Don't I?" I pushed the button for the fifth floor harder than I needed to. "What exactly don't I understand?"

"I mean I've had other people in my life, but..." He exhaled hard. "But there's never been another you. And believe me, I've looked."

I stared at him, completely mute.

Adam stepped back, giving me as much space as this tiny box would allow. "That's all I wanted to say."

My heart thundered. "Is that... Is that really all you wanted to say?"

"It's all I wanted to *say*, yes." He chewed his lip. "Can't promise it was all I wanted to do."

"What does that mean?"

Adam met my eyes. "Do I have to spell it out?"

"Humor me."

He took a step toward me, and my heart rate shot even higher. "I missed you, Dale. That was the whole reason I came to the reunion. To see you."

I swallowed hard. "Really?"

He nodded, and I couldn't breathe at all.

"There was no one else there I wanted to see," he said. "Not enough to fly across the country." He took a slow, cautious step closer to me. "Just you."

"Adam..."

He took another step, and we were nearly touching. Then he reached for my waist, and we *were* touching.

I pulled in as much air as I could, which wasn't much. "But after... It's been so long since...and I..."

"It's been *too* long." He leaned in closer, sending my heart rate soaring and turning my knees to water. "It's been way too long"—he touched my face—"and for that, I can never be sorry enough."

And he kissed me.

47

Chapter Four

One kiss, and I thought I was going to drop to my knees at Adam's feet.

He'd always been a phenomenal kisser. Even the very first time, when we were inexperienced kids kissing in the smoky dark, he'd known just how to make me weak. Now, as a bolder, more aggressive—no, more *confident*—adult, he liquefied me. His lips were soft and at the same time demanding, pushing mine apart so he had full access to my mouth. He cradled the back of my neck in his hand and tilted his head as he slipped his tongue between my lips and deepened the kiss.

God knew how long we went on before we finally came up for air. No one had ever been able to make me lose track of time and space like Adam did, and when we broke the kiss, it took me a moment to remember where I was.

Adam touched his forehead to mine. "I missed you."

"I missed you too." Deep down, I hated myself for admitting it to him, for giving in to this, but I *did* miss him. And I *did* want him.

His hand shook as he ran his fingers through my hair, and before I could even think to say anything else, he pressed his lips to mine again. He held me closer, grasping my hair as he teased my tongue with the tip of his. Just like he had ten and twenty years ago, he shook me right to the core with a kiss and a touch.

Except I knew better this time. Damn it, *I knew better*.

I put my hands on his chest and pushed myself away from him. "We can't do this. We shouldn't."

"Dale—"

"*I* can't." I pushed the button again, and the doors opened. "I need to go."

I stepped out of the elevator, and the son of a bitch followed me out into the hall.

"Dale, can we at least talk?" he asked. "After all this time, we should just—"

"We should just let it go." I faced him, arms folded across my chest because that was the only way I could keep them from visibly trembling. "We have talked. And if we keep talking, I'm going to do something I'll regret."

He stiffened. "I wouldn't ask you do something you didn't want to."

"I didn't say it was something I didn't want to do," I snapped. "Just that I'd regret it."

He took a half step back, which gave me some much-needed breathing room but also made me want to reach for him and close up that distance again.

"Look," he said. "I don't blame you for being hurt about the last couple of times. I really don't. And I'm not about to tell you to let it go after all these years, because I sure haven't."

My heart quickened again, but I didn't speak.

"I mean it, Dale," he whispered, his voice unsteady. "I came here to see you. Not to fuck you and then go home." He showed his palms as he inched closer to the elevator and farther from me. "I don't want to hurt you again. I don't want you to regret this. Not like the last couple of times."

"What do you want from this time?" I asked. "Sex?"

"Of course I want sex with you," he said. "But what I really want... I mean, that's not everything I..." He paused. "If I haven't been able to stop thinking about this after twenty fucking years, I—" He stopped abruptly and then exhaled and

49

shook his head. "Forget it. The one thing I don't want is to hurt you, so let's just quit while we're ahead."

"No, let's not." I shifted my weight, tightening my arms across my chest. "It took us twenty years to get here, so let's have it out."

"And accomplish *what*, exactly?" His sudden defensiveness startled me. "I didn't come here to give you another reason to think I'm a sleaze ball."

"Then why... Why did you come here?" I asked. "Just for sex? Or something more?"

Adam held my gaze for a long moment, and I couldn't tell if he looked scared, hurt, or a combination of the two. The military had hardened him and sharpened all his edges, but standing in front of me now, he was the vulnerable kid I'd known in high school. The jock who had more feelings than he knew what to do with.

He took a breath. "Do you *really* think I would come looking for you after twenty years *just* for sex?"

My throat constricted, but Adam didn't wait for an answer. He swore under his breath and reached for the elevator button.

"Wait." I lunged forward and grabbed his wrist.

He stared at me, eyes wide. "What?"

"Don't leave."

We locked eyes. Adam swallowed. My heart pounded.

"Let's..." I swept my tongue across my lips. "Let's go back to my room."

He blinked a few times. "Are you—"

"Shut up." I let go of his wrist and reached for the front of his shirt. "Just...just shut up. Talking isn't getting us anywhere."

I kissed him again, and he didn't argue. He hesitated but then wrapped his arms around me and surrendered to my kiss just like I'd surrendered to his. I had no idea what I was getting myself into, if this was a good idea or a terrible one, but kissing him like this and holding him against me felt right. Regrets could be dealt with tomorrow. I needed him today.

I broke the kiss and took his hand, and we hurried down the hall to my hotel room.

"Are you sure about this?" he asked as I pulled my card key out of my pocket.

Struggling to get the card into the reader, I said, "Yes. I am."

The reader finally took the key. The LED turned green. The latch clicked.

I opened the door, and Adam took over. Arm around my waist, he shoved me into the room and kicked the door shut behind us. He pinned me up against the wall, and I'd have gasped with both surprise and arousal, but he didn't give me a chance. One second we were moving, and the next, he was kissing me hard and violently, like only he had ever done. Our bodies ground together, our mouths ground together, and it bordered on painful—hell, it was painful—but it turned me on like nothing else.

I grabbed the front of his shirt and dragged him down onto the bed with me, not relinquishing my grip as I kissed him again. He slid a hand under the back of my head and closed his fingers around my hair, stinging my scalp as he returned my kiss with that violent, desperate fervor that turned me inside out.

His kiss was frantic and breathless, without a trace of insecurity or uncertainty. When I wrapped my legs around his waist, he groaned and pressed his hips against mine. Holy fuck, he was rock hard, and my whole body tingled at the memory of taking every inch of that thick cock.

He kissed my neck, his stubble scraping my skin. "I need... I need you naked."

I bit my lip. I'd forgotten he could be so blunt, even crass, in bed, and I'd forgotten how much I loved it.

He kissed my neck. Shoulder. Collarbone. His jaw was freshly shaved, but just coarse enough to lightly burn, and I bit my lip, squirming beneath him.

"God, Dale..." He nipped just above my collar, driving a whimper out of me. "It's been so long, I don't even know where I want to start."

I arched against him. "You're already off to a good start."

"I know, but I..." He sighed and pressed a warm kiss beneath my jaw. "So many things I want to do to you."

"Do it *all*," I breathed.

Adam shivered. "I want you. I want to fuck you."

"Please do," I murmured, and just the thought of having him inside me had me shaking and ready to come unglued. "Oh, fuck, Adam... Please..."

He kissed me lightly. "We should get these clothes off, then." As he started to push himself up, I grabbed his shirt.

"Half-dressed sex is hot," I said. "We should—"

"I want to see you," he whispered. "*All* of you."

My grip on his shirt melted away, and he sat up. So did I.

He tugged his shirt free from his waistband. I slid my hands under his shirt and pushed it up and off. Mine came off too, and once we were stripped to the waist, we just looked at each other for a moment.

God damn, but the military had chiseled him to a degree of perfection time hadn't even begun to temper. The contours of his muscles were smooth and defined, just begging for a fingertip or a tongue to trace their curves and lines.

Our eyes met again.

If his body was breathtaking, his eyes were beyond description. No wonder he still made me weak after all these years. His eyes said *I want you* and *we've got a lot of time to make up for* and *I'm going to make you come so hard you'll cry.*

Bring it on, Adam. I reached for his face, and as soon as I was close enough, he wrapped his arms around me. There was nothing tender about a kiss like this, nothing gentle or affectionate; this was all lust and need and *years* of pent-up hunger.

All at once, he broke the kiss, but before I could protest, he shoved me onto my back. Then he was over me, and he was kissing me again, his hot skin against mine. I shivered beneath him and dug my fingers into his shoulders as we made out across the mattress.

He shifted his weight onto one arm and reached between us with the other. The dull pressure of his fingers sliding across my clothed erection was fucking divine, and I raised my hips, pushing against him and seeking more. Adam grinned against my lips as he stroked me through my pants.

"We should... We should get these off." I felt around for his belt buckle. "Don't need any clothes."

"Mmm, no, we don't, do we?"

Both our belts jingled as we unbuckled them and pulled them free. He unzipped my pants, and I pressed against him, making my still-clothed erection rub against his fingers again. Adam grinned. Looking me right in the eye, he slid his hand over my cock, squeezing through my clothes.

"You really like that, don't you?"

"Of course I do." I licked my lips. "You're touching me."

"Not yet I'm not." He worked his fingers past my zipper and into the front of my boxers. When I gasped, he kissed me, and as he wrapped his hand around my cock, I almost lost my fucking mind.

And he didn't help at all when he whispered, "I want to fuck you, Dale."

"*Please.*"

He grinned and released me. "You have condoms with you?"

"Oh. Honey." I kissed him again. "You'd better believe I have condoms."

He pressed his hard cock against me, and in a low, spine-tingling growl, said, "You might want to get them. Like now."

"Then you'd better get out of those pants," I murmured.

"Likewise."

We stripped off the rest of our clothes, and then I leaned over the bed and yanked the zipper on my suitcase. After riffling around for a second, I found the condoms and lube I'd made sure to pack.

"You came well-prepared," he said with a grin.

"Of course I did."

As I handed him a square of gold foil, he arched an eyebrow and smirked. "Magnums, eh?"

"Oh, I have others with me." I waved a hand at my bag. "For the less fortunate."

"Well this"—he plucked it from between my fingers—"will do just fine."

"Yes, I know."

We exchanged grins. Then he put on the condom, and I covered it in lube. When I was finished, he poured some more lube onto his hand, and I whimpered as he smoothed it onto his fingers.

"Just skip that part," I said, barely managing to enunciate. "I want—"

"You'll wait." His hand drifted up my inner thigh, and I parted my legs for him. "We're doing things my way."

I wanted to protest, to beg, plead, demand that he fuck me right this second, but his fingertip teased me just then, and all I could do was whimper.

"That's what I thought," he said with the most devilish grin in his voice. He slid a finger into me. The lube made sure it was slick and smooth, but he used just enough force to add a little friction and create the slightest, most delicious burn.

"Just *fuck* me, for God's sake."

"Oh, I will." He added a second finger, slowly pushing both of them into me. "But I love making you squirm first."

"You are such a—*ooh*, God..."

He beckoned against that sweet spot inside. "Such a what? I didn't catch that."

I gripped the bedclothes on either side of me, arching and squirming as he fucked me with his fingers.

"That drive you crazy?" he asked with a devilish grin. "Taking my fingers while my cock is all hard and ready—"

I reached up and grabbed the back of his neck and pulled him down into a demanding kiss. As I did, he curved his fingers just right and found my prostate again, and I broke that kiss with a gasp. "Adam, for fuck's sake..."

He withdrew his fingers and shoved me roughly onto my stomach. His knee forced my legs apart, and I almost came from anticipation alone as he picked up the bottle of lube again. The bottle clicked, then again, and when it dropped onto the bed beside me, I pressed my forehead into the mattress, holding my breath and trying not to lose my mind.

Adam guided his dick to me. I spread my legs farther and pressed my ass up against him, seeking that pressure, that burn, and we both sighed as the head of his cock pushed into me. He wasn't gentle or careful, not unduly forceful, just the right side of demanding and aggressive. He'd prepped me well, and the burn, the stretch, it was enough to make my eyes water, and my God it felt *spectacular.*

Bedclothes gathered in my clawing fingers. As Adam picked up speed, thrusting into me hard enough to make my eyes water, the whole bed shifted beneath us. Every thrust not only forced him deep inside me but rubbed my own cock against the comforter beneath me.

He kissed my shoulder. "Am I hurting you?"

"You will be if you fuck me any harder," I said.

"Is that an invitation?"

"More like a challenge."

"Oh yeah?" He thrust in deep and hard. "Challenge accepted."

There was no witty comment on the tip of my tongue. No comeback. I was helpless, surrendered, completely at his mercy, and I was so deep in this ecstasy I couldn't begin to form a coherent thought.

And Adam couldn't have picked a better angle to fuck me. His cock slid past my prostate and blurred my vision, and with every thrust, my own cock rubbed even more against the comforter, and the combined friction drove me insane. Having him inside me drove me insane. My God, this was so incredible I couldn't take it. I bucked up against him, taking as much of him as I could, and released a helpless cry as I came. He kept forcing himself into me, groaning as he fucked me right through the peak of my orgasm, and then he thrust into me as deep as I could take him, groaned again, and shuddered.

Adam kissed the back of my neck. Then he withdrew. As he sat up, I rolled onto my back, and then he leaned down to kiss me full-on. It was a less demanding kiss now, a breathless one, and we just let our tongues lazily intertwine as we caressed each other with hot, unsteady hands.

He lifted himself up on his forearms and met my eyes. My heart was beating wildly now, and it had nothing to do with the sex or the orgasm or the exertion. I reached up to brush a drop of sweat from his temple.

"I didn't think it was possible," he murmured, "but you're even better than you were ten years ago."

"Likewise."

We cleaned ourselves up and returned to the disheveled bed. He pulled me into his arms, and he kissed me, and judging by the way we kissed, this *wasn't* going to be a fuck and run. A one-night stand, maybe, but I didn't see either of us putting on any clothes for a while.

I broke the kiss just enough to ask, "When does your flight leave?"

"I have to be at the airport at nine thirty tomorrow." He dipped his head and kissed his way down my neck. "What about yours?"

"Tomorrow afternoon." I shivered as I pulled in a breath. "Want to stay tonight?"

"You'd better believe it," he growled and lifted up so he could kiss my mouth again.

All my reservations from earlier weren't gone, but they tucked themselves into the back of my mind. I'd deal with them later.

Maybe I'd regret this tomorrow, maybe I wouldn't, but right now, his kiss was intoxicating, and his body was hot against mine. Sex with him had always been second to none, and even after nothing more than a quick, sweaty fuck, I was aching for more.

Tomorrow, we'd go our separate ways. Tonight? Tonight I'd indulge in sex with the man I'd fantasized about since we were teenagers.

He broke the kiss. Stroking my face with the backs of his fingers, he said, "How many condoms did you bring?"

"Enough to keep us busy until you leave for the airport."

His devilish grin gave me goose bumps, especially when he asked, "Is that an invitation?"

I slid closer to him, molding my body to his. "More like a challenge."

"Challenge accepted."

Chapter Five

Standing in the security line at the airport, I could barely move. I wasn't hungover, but I sure felt like I was. My head throbbed. My body ached.

Yesterday and last night were scorching hot. All three times. We might not have been twenty-eight or eighteen anymore, but neither of us was lacking in stamina. And then this morning? Spectacular. Nothing quite like being pinned up against the shower wall and mercilessly fucked until we both came so hard we could barely stand.

Five stars. Perfect score. Gold medal. Two thumbs up.

And yep, I regretted the fuck out of it.

Pity I wasn't hungover. At least then I could blame last night on being stupid drunk instead of knowing damn well I went into it fully sober, ready and willing to beg if it came down to it.

He talked a good game out in the hallway. I'd swallowed up every word just like I'd swallowed every inch of that beautiful cock after we'd showered again last night.

Hadn't I promised myself I wouldn't sleep with him again? And hadn't Rhett warned me not to get into bed with Adam again?

On the other hand, there was no expectation beyond last night. Or, well, this morning. No promise of something more. No stringing each other along until the truth reared its ugly head and ended things before they started. Again.

We also lived twelve hundred miles apart. He was stationed in San Diego. I lived in Seattle. Seeing each other again required plane tickets and either time off work or traveling for a weekend and being exhausted and miserable on Monday.

"Next, please!" The sharp voice jarred me out of my thoughts, and I moved up to the podium where a TSA agent who looked as tired as I was examined tickets and IDs. He stamped my ticket and waved me past.

I went through all the motions at the security checkpoint. Shoes off, laptop out, backpack in the tray, make sure to give the guy with the scanner a flirty look so he definitely did *not* pick me out for the random grope, things gathered, shoes back on. I didn't fly very often, and every time I did, it only took this part to remind me why I preferred to drive, take the train, or just stay home. Maybe I should have thought about that before I booked this trip.

I shouldered my laptop case and went in search of a cup of coffee. Twenty years in Seattle had turned me into a goddamned addict, and I needed my fix before I got on the plane. A coffee snob too, but running on only a few hours of sleep and with a flight ahead of me, I'd take what I could get.

Coffee in hand, I strolled down the concourse to my gate. When I got there, it wasn't terribly crowded, so I found a seat by the window and watched planes come and go while I sipped my so-so coffee.

And as it often did when I was idle, my mind wandered. Back to this morning, back to last night, and then even further back, to another hotel ballroom under another banner welcoming back the class of nineteen-ninety-mumble. And there was Adam, getting a beer from the bar, looking a little younger than he did last night and a hell of a lot hotter than he had that night after graduation.

We met up. Handshake, small talk, all of that bullshit.

And then he'd asked, "So are you...here with anyone?"

I'd shaken my head. "Boyfriend and I split a few months ago. So, it's just me."

"Oh. Sorry to hear it."

"He was a douche," I'd said with a dismissive shrug. "Good riddance." Pause. "What about you? Are you, um, with anyone?""

"I'm, well..." He'd blown out a breath. "On paper, married."

To this day, I could feel how hard the "married" part had hit me in the gut. "On paper?"

"Yeah. We're separated. Things were good for a while, but..." Adam shook his head.

"Sorry to hear it," I said.

Adam shrugged. "It happens. We're meeting to discuss the actual divorce after I get back." Into his beer bottle, he added, "I can't *wait* until that's over."

So the door was open. We were both unattached, and while everyone around us talked about kids and jobs and everything they'd done in the last ten years, we danced around the tension that an unexpected one-night stand had long ago left between us. The tension that had weathered all those years while our classmates earned degrees and had babies, hadn't even begun to die.

We went outside for a cigarette, even though I had stopped smoking by then. A breath of fresh air, I guess. Then we walked, we talked, and at some point, Adam kissed me, and I didn't stand a chance.

The next morning, we exchanged phone numbers at the airport. We didn't kiss good-bye. Not out in public. But I wasn't worried. We'd make up for that the next time we saw each other.

Two days after we'd both flown back to our respective cities—he was stationed in Norfolk at the time—he called. We talked about hotels and plane tickets, and I could hear the grin in his voice that mirrored mine as we made plans to meet up again in the next month or so.

But two weeks after that, he called me again. Nothing about planes and hotels this time. Apparently the meeting to discuss divorce terms had taken an unexpected turn. I never could recall his exact words, just the crushing sensation of the truth and the effort it took to make him believe I was happy for him and that I wished him and Jackie the best. We'd keep in touch. We'd stay friends. He owed it to his wife to give it one more try.

We didn't stay in touch, though. And now that we'd reconnected, I didn't find the least bit of smug satisfaction in learning that their attempt to repair their marriage had failed. If anything, I wanted to be angry with the two of them for not getting it together. If resuscitating that marriage was the reason Adam had to let me go, then they damn well better have given it everything they had before calling time on it.

I shook myself back to life and watched a plane touch down on the runway outside.

It was over. Last night, both reunions, the first time; they were all over. And it occurred to me that we'd never made any definitive plans to stay in touch after this reunion. There were no expectations now. No promises to break. No inevitable awkward letdowns. We'd spent a hot night together and settled a few things, and neither of us had suggested anything would happen after we left.

I pulled my phone out of my pocket and scrolled through my contacts to Adam's name. I hesitated, and then pressed the "delete contact" button.

Do you want to permanently delete Adam O'Connor?

Without another moment's hesitation, I pressed *Delete*.

Contact deleted.

I smiled, slid the phone back into my pocket, and sat back. There. Done. We'd talked things through, buried the hatchet and then spent a few hours naked in bed. Couldn't think of a better way to put twenty years to rest. Now he was behind me, and I could move on.

Finally.

As soon as the plane touched down in Seattle, everyone had their phones out, myself included.

I had a text from Kieran: *Are you back in town today? Want to join Alex and me for dinner?*

Dinner that didn't require cooking or calling? Hell yeah. I quickly sent back, *Just landed. Should be home by six.*

While I was at it, I also sent Rhett a quick text: *Back in town. Movie night sometime this week?*

I put my phone away and waited for the passengers ahead of me to gather their things and move off the plane.

My phone buzzed again.

Kieran had written back, *See you tonight. Our place, six thirty. Bring nothing.*

Sounds good, I sent back.

Then my stomach tightened. I sometimes hung out with Alex and Kieran on their own, rather than just with Rhett and Ethan, but I remembered now that Kieran had mentioned something recently about hooking me up with one of the bartenders from Wilde's, the infamous den of debauchery where Kieran worked and most hot gay men in town went to get laid.

Not that I'd object to that. The bartenders at Wilde's were pure unadulterated sex on wheels. It was pretty much a requirement to work there. And management, being the saints they were, required all the bartenders to wear tux shirts and bowties. There wasn't a man behind that bar I wouldn't let fuck me within an inch of my life. One after the other, thank you very much.

And if I had any lingering feelings for Adam, any regrets or resentment that might come bubbling up as time went on, maybe that bartender from Wilde's would be just the ticket for moving on.

Alex and Kieran had a small but lovely apartment on Capitol Hill, a couple of blocks off Broadway. Walking distance to Kieran's job at Wilde's and a short drive to Alex's classes at the University of Washington. Bonus? It was only a few blocks away from the condo I'd bought last year.

"So how was the reunion?" Alex asked as we lounged on their couch with a few glasses of merlot.

I shrugged. "Typical of a reunion."

He raised his eyebrows. "You're speaking to someone who's never attended one, remember?"

"Ooh, right. I forgot you've only been out of kindergarten since last year."

Kieran snickered.

"Hey." Alex wagged a finger at him. "Watch it. You're not that much older than me."

"No, I'm not." Kieran gave him a significant look. "I hope you'll remember that next time you're cracking over-the-hill jokes about me."

"Nope, probably not," Alex said with a shrug.

"You're impossible."

I laughed. "You have no one to blame but yourself, Kieran, darling. He was sweet and polite until you got your hands on him."

"He's right, you know." Alex batted his eyes at Kieran.

Chuckling, Kieran put an arm around Alex's waist and kissed his cheek. "Brat."

"To answer your question," I said, "the reunion was...interesting."

"Was it worth going?" Kieran asked.

I swirled my wine for a second. Then I nodded. "Yeah, it was worth it. Caught up with some people I hadn't seen in far too long."

Alex elbowed Kieran. "You sure you don't want to go to yours?"

Kieran eyed him. "You still want to do that weekend in Vegas before we get married?"

"Point taken. Never mind. No reunion."

"That's what I thought." Kieran looked at me. "You're invited to that, by the way. First week of August."

"Vegas?" I grinned, thankful for the shift away from the topic of my reunion. "Don't tell me you two are eloping."

Alex laughed. "No. But Kieran and Ethan are both convinced it wouldn't be right for me to get married when I haven't at least had one weekend of partying in Vegas, and Rhett's insisting on chaperoning."

"Wise men." I raised my glass. "Good on you for listening to them."

Kieran picked up the wine bottle and topped off his glass. As he offered the bottle to me, he asked, "So, are you in?"

"For the wine or the weekend?"

He rolled his eyes. "Both, idiot."

"Of course I'm in." I held out my glass, and as he poured a little more, I added, "You should know I'd never turn down a weekend of sin."

"Didn't think so," Alex said, chuckling. He held out his glass to Kieran.

"So have you heard from Rhett and Ethan since you got back?" Kieran asked as he filled Alex's glass.

"Uh, no," I said. "Should I have?"

"You probably will sooner or later," Alex said. "Rhett's kind of coming unglued because that kid *finally* proposed to Sabrina."

"He did? Good Lord, it certainly took him long enough."

"No kidding." Kieran laughed. "But you should see Ethan. I think knowing their daughter is getting married is giving him a midlife crisis."

"Another one?" I clicked my tongue and shook my head. "That man is seriously abusing the privilege."

Kieran and Alex both laughed.

I took another drink and then set my glass on a coaster on the coffee table. "Now, let's get down to important topics, here. Tell me more about this bartender you two keep trying to set me up with."

Kieran grinned. "He's fucking hot."

Alex whistled. "He so is."

"Kieran. Alex." I huffed and rolled my eyes. "He works at Wilde's. Of course he's hot. Tell me something I *don't* know."

In a stage whisper, Alex said, "Mention the accent."

"Accent?" I sat up. "Do tell."

Kieran laughed. "He's from South Carolina. Has that gorgeous Southern drawl."

I put a hand to my chest. "Ooh, I'm listening. Wilde's and a Southern accent. Where do I sign?"

"You want to see a picture of him first?"

I answered with nothing more than a pointed look.

"Right. Picture." Kieran pulled up a picture on his phone. "Ah, here he is. I give you...Owen." He turned it so I could see the screen.

Oh dear sweet mother of God. Yes, that man had been blessed. The picture was taken at Wilde's—I knew that background *quite* well—and he was dressed for work: tailored tux pants, a white shirt, and a bowtie and cummerbund. Clean-cut, chiseled from marble, meticulously styled brown hair, and overall absolutely gorgeous.

I gestured at the picture. "And you're telling me *that* has a Southern accent?"

"Indeed he does."

"Oh my Lord." I shook my head. "That's entirely too much hot in one package."

Kieran's lips pulled back in a devilish grin. "So does that mean you're interested?"

"Hmm." I stroked my chin. Owen was hot, and I certainly had a weak spot for that type of accent, but truth be told, he didn't pique my interest as much as he should have. Though I *was* tired from traveling, not to mention still aching from being fucked good and hard last night. And again this morning. Fatigue could've been what was putting a damper on my enthusiasm.

"Give him my number," I said. "I'd love to meet up with him."

"There's a shock." Alex looked at Kieran. "And if it doesn't work out with them, we can invite him for a threesome, right?"

"Oh, hell," I said. "Why wait? Make it a foursome. I'll bring wine and porn."

Kieran shivered. "I do love the way you think, Dale."

As evenings always did, this one wound to a close. We said our good-byes, and I headed home.

Walking back to my condo, I pulled out my phone to take it off silent mode. As I did, a message flashed onto the screen:

1 Missed Call.

I sighed. *Damn it, Rhett. When will you ever get the hang of texting? Just tell me tonight or tomorrow, for heaven's sake.*

I hit the button, and as soon as the number appeared, my heart skipped. It was an unknown number, but the first three digits were familiar. I didn't have to Google it. Deep down, I knew it was a San Diego area code.

Cringing inwardly, I called my voice mail, entered the password and waited.

"Dale, hey, it's Adam. Give me a call back, okay?"

Typical Adam. Short and sweet. He never did like talking to recordings.

Blood pounding in my ears, I stopped on the sidewalk and stared at my now silent phone. He didn't like talking to recordings, and I wasn't so sure I wanted to talk to him. Okay, I did. Of course I did. Whether or not it was a good idea, though, that was up for debate.

Lead me not into temptation…

I waited until I got home before I returned his call.

He picked up on the first ring. "Dale, hey."

"Hey." *What the hell am I doing?* "You called?"

"Yeah." He paused. Movement in the background suggested he was getting comfortable. Maybe sitting down or leaning back in a chair or something. "I, um…"

I chewed my lip, drumming my fingers on the armrest of the couch while I waited for him to untie his tongue.

He took a breath. "Listen, I was thinking on the way home today, and...I want to stay in touch this time." He paused. "But as, you know, as friends."

Only Adam could possibly make my heart flutter with excitement at the same time he hit me in the gut.

"Just friends? Don't you think it might be a little difficult to go back to that after we've..." I closed my eyes. I never had trouble compartmentalizing sex and everything else. Hell, I'd fucked the same coworker at three Christmas parties in a row, and we'd never batted an eye at each other afterward. But with Adam...

"At least to start with," Adam said. "I don't want to lose touch with you again, but I also don't want something to blow up in our faces."

I chewed the inside of my cheek. I didn't want this to blow up in our faces either, but I wasn't entirely confident in my ability to look at Adam and not touch. We may have only crossed that line a few times, but all it took was once with someone like him.

Still, having him in my life as a friend was better than not having him in my life at all.

"All right," I said. "I guess we'll see how 'just friends' goes."

And I hoped to God I wasn't signing myself up for a heaping dose of heartache.

Chapter Six

True to our word, Adam and I stayed in touch. E-mails and the odd phone call became more frequent e-mails and longer phone calls. Now and then, we chatted on the webcam, which was nice. I couldn't imagine ever getting tired of seeing his face and hearing his voice.

Maybe we could pull off this "just friends" business. Things were less awkward now, at least. Sex had happened, it had been acknowledged, and I didn't feel quite so much like we were ignoring it now. Rather, we just had other things to talk about, and it never came up.

What did come up, though, was the fact that because Adam was retiring from the navy in a few months, he was job hunting and had looked into several of the various naval bases that hired civilian contractors for different jobs. Me and my big mouth, I reminded him that there was a shipyard in Bremerton, which was only an hour by ferry from Seattle. He'd already been looking into the naval base in Everett to the north and contacted Bremerton too. As luck would have it, he managed to get interviews at both facilities during the same week.

And now, three weeks after the reunion, here I was sitting in my car in the Sea-Tac Airport cell phone lot, waiting for Adam to text me to say he was on the ground.

Here. In Seattle.

On my turf.

Apparently this was the week I'd find out if we could pull off this whole "just friends" thing when we were face-to-face. Adam seemed confident we could. I was...cautiously optimistic.

My phone buzzed on the dashboard, so I picked it up.

Just got to baggage claim. Meet you outside.

Be there shortly. I sent the text back and put my car in gear.

Whether or not this was a good idea was about to be a moot point, so I tried to push my worries to the back of my mind. Emphasis on *tried.* My heart beat faster and faster as I inched along under the names of the various airlines.

And there he was.

One glance sent a full-body shiver through me. Naturally, he looked good. He must've just had a haircut, because the sides were shaved almost to the skin and the top was short and sharp. Still long enough to lie flat instead of standing up like a buzz cut or something, but shorter than the last time I'd seen him.

He smiled, and I returned it, and oh God, I was going to spend four days with him?

Okay, so maybe not four whole days. I had to work part of the time, and he had his interviews, and... Fuck, I was going to lose my mind.

Just friends, Dale. Remember? No pressure. No pretenses.

Just. Friends.

I stopped beside the curb. Adam put his bag in the backseat and then got in on the passenger side.

"How was your flight?" I asked as I pulled back into traffic.

"Not bad," he said. "Short, thank God. Thought it was going to be delayed, but whatever issue they were having, they fixed it quickly."

"Well, it's a good thing you landed when you did," I said. "We should miss most of the traffic getting back into the city."

"Traffic? It's not even two o'clock."

"Yeah, but Boeing lets out at two. And believe me, that is not a traffic jam you want to get into if you can avoid it."

"Ouch."

"Ouch is right. And about the time that mess clears up, everyone else is getting off work, and it's just a massive clusterfuck." *Why am I rambling about traffic?* I cleared my throat. "So, um, what's your schedule like while you're here? I could probably take a day off from work if you want to do some sightseeing."

Adam smiled. "That would be fun. I've got a fair amount of time, actually. I have an interview on Monday morning at the shipyard in Bremerton and another one at the base in Everett that afternoon."

I grimaced. "You might want to reschedule one or the other."

"Oh?"

"Seattle's an hour by ferry from Bremerton, and you're looking at easily an hour to get to Everett from Seattle. If there's an accident somewhere on the freeway—and I promise you, there will be—it'll take twice as long."

"Oh. Shit."

"Any way you can reschedule it?"

He blew out a breath. "I can certainly try. Thanks for the heads up."

"Any time."

The freeway was, as I'd predicted, mostly clear. As downtown Seattle came into view, with buildings shooting up from behind the snarl of interstates and overpasses, a weird feeling twisted in my gut. This city had been my home for twenty years, and it was strange to see Adam here. Like he didn't quite jive with the backdrop of mountains and skyscrapers.

Or maybe it was me. That was probably it, because I wasn't sure how I felt about him bleeding into this world.

Adam rested an elbow below the window and glanced at me. "By the way, are you, um, sure about this? Having me stay with you instead of at a hotel?"

"Of course." I gestured dismissively. "I've got a guest room, so why make you pay for a hotel room?"

He eyed me.

I sighed. "We agreed we're just friends, right?"

Adam nodded. "Right. I just don't want things getting awkward between us."

Probably a little too late for that. The fact that my guest room was cheaper, more comfortable and probably a hell of a lot quieter than any decent hotel in town was moot when we took into consideration how close it was to *my bed.*

There was no turning back now, though, and about an hour after I picked him up, I let us into my condo.

Adam looked around. "Wow, this is a really nice place."

"Thanks."

I showed him down the short hall to the guest bedroom.

He set his bag on the bed. "You mind if I grab a quick shower?" He waved a hand at his clothes. "I always feel like such a wreck after I've been flying."

"Sure, go right ahead."

While he settled in and headed for the shower, I went into the kitchen. It was a little early for a glass of wine, but whatever.

The shower turned on in the other room, and my glass of wine was gone in a single gulp. It was five o'clock somewhere. Adam O'Connor was naked in my bathroom. I didn't care what time it was.

As I poured my second glass, I glanced down the hall in Adam's general direction. My mind's eye naturally filled in everything I couldn't see, and I shivered. I wondered if he'd let me join him in there and quickly banished the thought, no matter how tempting it was. It was dangerous to even let myself fantasize with no intention of following through, because I wanted to follow through. We shouldn't, so I wouldn't.

Rationally, I knew we were doing the right thing. Sex between us was amazing, but I'd missed our friendship for far too long to quite literally fuck it away. Adam meant more to me than the orgasms we gave each other.

I wouldn't cross any lines this week. I'd stay true to my word that this was friendship and nothing more. I'd keep my hands to myself.

No matter how much wine it took.

That evening, I took him downtown to one of my favorite restaurants. The food was good—it was basically a bar and grill masquerading as a hipster bistro—but it was the view that kept me coming back time and again. The massive picture windows looked out on the sparkling waters of Puget Sound. There were a few cargo ships anchored in the water out by Alki Point, and one of the green-and-white car ferries left a long V-shaped wake as it made another slow, steady run toward Bainbridge Island or Bremerton.

We placed our orders and then sat back, and for a long moment, we both just looked out the window, watching the sun sink behind the Olympic Mountains on the other side of the glittering Sound.

He cradled his wineglass between two fingers. "This is a beautiful city. Not nearly as gray as I thought it would be."

"The rain's not as bad as people say it is. Quite nice most of the time, actually."

"So what ultimately made you stay here?" he asked. "I mean, I thought you were just coming here to go to college, and then..."

"Found a job." I shrugged. "And I just liked it here. Hell, look at it." I gestured out at the water.

Nodding, he smiled. "Yeah, I can sure see the attraction."

"It's not a bad place. So do you really think you might take one of those jobs up here?"

Adam shrugged, shifting his gaze toward the darkening mountains. "I don't know. I'll have enough to live off for a while after I retire, but I'm just not sure what I want to do yet or where I want to go."

"Well, it's not a bad area," I said. "If you can deal with the traffic and the fact that the whole city goes into a panic if anyone even mentions snow."

He laughed and looked at me across the table. "Every city has its pros and cons."

"That's true." I gestured out at the city and the Sound. "This place has a lot of cons, but once you're here, it kind of grows on you."

"Like mold?"

"More like moss."

Adam chuckled. "Well, maybe it'll grow on me after a while. I like what I've seen of it so far."

Our eyes met. My heart skipped. I had a feeling this conversation was going to get the wrong kind of emotional if we didn't shift gears in a hurry. "So, um, you still a baseball fan?"

"Am I still a baseball fan?" He shot me an incredulous look. "That's like asking if I'm still a fan of sex or breathing."

"I should have known."

He chuckled. "My first wife thought I was—"

"Wait, wait, wait." I shook my head. "First wife? I thought you were only married once."

Adam's cheeks colored. "I... No."

I raised an eyebrow. "How many ex-Mrs. O'Connors *are* there?"

"Um, well..." The color in his face deepened.

"Adam..."

He cleared his throat and held up three fingers.

My jaw dropped. "You've been married *three times*?"

Adam nodded. "Yep."

"Wow." I swirled my wine. "Okay, now I'm curious. Tell me about these women and why they aren't Mrs. O'Connor anymore."

He laughed softly. "Well, the common denominator is me, so..."

"Yeah, but it takes two to tango, as they say."

"True. It does." He drained his wineglass. He poured himself some more and offered the bottle to me. Once he'd topped us both off, he sat back and took a deep breath. "Hailey and I were on a ship together, and she was coming up due for orders. We were still in that madly in love phase, and..." He trailed off, laughing quietly. "We were young, stupid, infatuated, and we couldn't stand the idea of one of us getting orders someplace else. So we got married."

"Wow." I slid my thumb up and down the stem of my wineglass. "How long did that last?"

"We divorced two years after we got married." Shaking his head, he looked out the window. "Probably should've done it a lot sooner. Well, I mean, we shouldn't have gotten married at all, but..." He shook his head again, and then sipped his wine.

"Anyway. Then there was Jackie. The one I was married to when—" His eyes flicked toward me.

"Right. The last reunion." I took a drink, wondering when the lovely wine in my glass had turned quite so fucking bitter.

"We lasted almost seven years." Adam sighed. "Probably about four years longer than we should have."

How convenient.

"Kristina and I met about six months before Jackie and I finally called it quits. We didn't get involved with each other until the papers were signed, and really, we should have known it wouldn't work."

"Why's that?" I asked.

"Do rebound relationships ever work?"

Wow, now who sounds bitter?

"Hmm, no," I said. "I suppose they don't."

We both fell silent. So instead of a potentially awkward conversation that might draw attention to that fact that Adam and I were together, we'd gone down this road instead. Yeah. Totally an improvement. Great going, Dale.

I wanted to derail the discussion in favor of a lighter subject, but curiosity was killing me. "Can I ask something personal?"

"Shoot."

I hesitated, swirling my wine just to give myself something to look at instead of him. "When you got married each time, did you think it would work? Or did you have, like, an inkling that it wouldn't?"

Adam let out a long breath. "I'm not sure I really thought about it, to be honest."

"What do you mean?"

"I mean, it just seemed like the right thing to do at the time. I was in love with each of them and couldn't imagine being

77

with anyone else. I didn't question how I'd feel in five or ten years. I didn't think about what it really meant to commit to someone for the rest of my life. I guess I went into marriage like it was a romantic gesture and a way of telling someone I loved them, rather than an actual commitment to stay with them forever."

"Interesting," I said and looked out at the darkening sky. Three failed marriages in twenty years. Not much of a sense of commitment even when he was walking down the aisle.

Much as I'd pined after him for all this time and was still physically attracted to him like *whoa*, I suddenly couldn't help thinking maybe I'd dodged a bullet after all.

Chapter Seven

Adam managed to reschedule one of his interviews so he wouldn't have to scramble from Bremerton to Everett. On Adam's last day in town, I took off from work and showed him around town, taking him to all the tourist spots, naturally. We went up to the observation deck of the Space Needle. When we went to Fremont, he joked that the Fremont Troll reminded him of his ex-mother-in-law—I didn't ask which one. We wandered around Capitol Hill, checking out the various shops and restaurants. Not Wilde's, though. Taking a hot man into a meat market like that would've been asking for trouble.

We spent the latter part of the afternoon wandering around Pike Place Market. That was a tourist staple if ever there was one. No trip to Seattle was complete without watching the various street performers or seeing the guys at the fish market tossing salmon.

"Wow, they really do have some good seafood here," Adam said, looking over the various catches of the day displayed on white beds of ice.

"Best in the area."

In fact, the halibut looked perfect today, and the price wasn't as ridiculous as it sometimes was.

I glanced at Adam. "We could stay in tonight, if you'd like." I gestured at the halibut. "I could cook."

"Cook?" He smirked. "*You?*"

I scoffed. "Why is that so shocking?"

"Um, well, because we were in the same home ec class in junior high and have the dental work to prove it?"

"I *beg* your pardon." I glared playfully at him. "I was fourteen. I've refined my technique a bit since then, thank you very much."

"Have you?" He chuckled. "This I gotta see. All right, let's do dinner in. I'll buy, you cook."

"Oh, you're buying?" I flashed him a grin. "Well in that case—"

"I'm on a navy salary, my friend. Don't push your luck."

"Point taken."

I bought two halibut steaks and picked up a few fresh vegetables for the side. I thought about getting a bottle of wine, but who was I kidding? Tiny condo be damned, I had enough wine to last me through Armageddon.

We headed back to my place, and I got to work preparing dinner.

I had a bar-style counter in my kitchen, which made it easy for us to carry on a conversation while I sliced and seasoned. Adam sat opposite me, and of course, we each had a glass of wine. It was a wonder the man didn't think I was an alcoholic with my giant, well-stocked wine rack and the fact that I nearly always had a glass in hand when he was around. So I liked a good wine? That didn't mean his presence had anything to do with why I was consuming it faster than I usually did. Or the fact that I was half tempted to hook up an IV of Chablis.

"What do you think our high school selves would think if they could see us now?" Adam asked out of the blue. Before I could read some deeper meaning into the question, he held up his wineglass, turning it between his fingers like some baffling treasure from another world. "Being able to get booze without worrying about getting carded. Hell, having a stockpile of it." He tilted the glass toward the densely populated rack.

I laughed as I busied myself organizing spices and utensils. "I don't think our high school selves would believe it. Especially the part where we're living on our own, getting up at the crack of dawn to work and not smoking every chance we get."

"Hmm, yeah. Good point." He took a sip of wine and rolled it around in his mouth for a moment. "You ever miss it?"

"What? Smoking?"

Adam chuckled. "No. High school."

"Oh. Jesus fuck, no."

"Really?" His tone shifted to an unusually nostalgic one. "I sometimes do."

"You do?" I snorted. "Do I need to remind you of all the bullshit we were glad to leave behind?"

He shook his head. "But what about the good stuff?"

"Such as?"

Our eyes met.

Oh. Right. That. My heart managed to speed up and sink lower in my chest at the same time.

"To be honest," he said quietly, "I think the toughest thing about moving on after high school was not having my partner in crime anymore."

I was missing more than my partner in crime. I took a deeper swallow of wine than was probably necessary. "Well, it only took twenty years, but we found each other again."

"Yeah. We did." Adam smiled, possibly more to himself than me, and gazed into his wineglass as he swirled it slowly. "You remember that summer we tried to build a boat for the race at the state fair?"

"Tried?" I laughed. "We had a flawless design, my friend. Not my fault someone wasn't patient enough to let the epoxy do its thing before sealing the cracks."

Adam's cheeks colored a little. "True, true. But that was a brilliant design. If you'd had a competent builder, you probably would've won the race."

"Maybe." I smiled. "But the ten weeks of building it was the fun part anyway."

"Even with someone who didn't understand complex things like epoxy putty?"

I laughed into my glass. "Yeah. Even with that." I took a sip, then pushed the glass away and started cutting up a tomato to put on the salad. "That was a great summer."

"It was. When I say I miss high school sometimes, that's the kind of stuff I mean."

Our eyes met again.

I broke eye contact and focused on cutting the tomato. "Me too. I miss things like that. The rest of high school, that can just"—*you're rambling, darling*—"not the rest of high school."

We reminisced a little about those days, about all the things we did in between dealing with the stress and drama of high school. Looking back, it was a small wonder my parents— and probably Adam's—had gone prematurely gray. The speeding tickets before the signatures were dry on our licenses. The ill-judged bonfire that almost burned my dad's tool shed down. Sneaking out, sneaking booze, sneaking smokes. It wasn't that we'd been bad kids, we'd just had the high energy of teenagers without the common sense of adults.

And the more I thought about it, the more I had to agree with Adam. I missed those days. I missed my partner in crime.

"So," he said after a while. "I'm curious about something."

"Yeah?"

He hesitated. "I've told you my sob stories about my ex-wives. What about you?"

Oh to hell with it. Let's put some Grey Goose in that IV.

I looked up from seasoning the halibut. "Adam, I'm pretty sure I don't need to tell you that I of all people have never had a wife, ex or otherwise."

He chuckled. "You know what I mean. Boyfriends?"

I lowered my gaze to the fish I was preparing. "A few."

"I... Is that a touchy nerve?" he asked, the humor gone from his voice. "I didn't mean to pry or anything. Just curious what you've been doing the last twenty years."

"Or *who* I've been doing?" I arched an eyebrow. After the words came out, I realized they sounded a lot cattier than I'd intended. Sighing, I focused on the fish again. "It's not that touchy, I just... Well, let's just say I kind of have a penchant for wanting guys I can't have."

"Is that right?"

"Yep. I'd never be a home wrecker or anything like that; I just have this terrible knack for getting infatuated with men who are either unavailable or so not the man I should get involved with."

Adam held my gaze. My heart jumped as I realized he was one of those men.

I quickly cleared my throat. "For example, I had the worst crush on my friend Rhett when I first met him. My God."

"And he was unavailable?"

I nodded. "Of course, he and his man split up for a while, but he was just such a wreck during that time, and I didn't want to be his rebound. Or ruin a friendship, you know?"

"I can understand that."

We locked eyes.

Awkwardness in three...two...

"So when did you learn to actually cook?" he asked suddenly.

I picked up the pan of fish to transfer it to the oven. "After the third time I got food poisoning in college."

"Oh my God. Really?"

"Yep. The takeout places near my apartment were..." I grimaced and shuddered. I shut the oven door, set the timer and turned around to wash my hands. Over my shoulder, I said, "It didn't help that I had a roommate who could turn macaroni and cheese into a three-day hospital stay, so I decided it was time to take matters into my own hands."

"Wise idea," Adam said. "Just be glad you've never eaten on a ship."

"That bad?"

"Ugh, it's awful. And the worst part? I can't even eat steak and lobster together anymore without getting horrible anxiety."

"What? Did they fuck it up that bad?"

Adam shook his head. "No, but one thing you learn very quickly in the navy is that when you're on cruise, steak and lobster means bad news."

"How so?"

"Any time the mess decks served them, we were getting bad news. Deployment was being extended or a liberty port was canceled. Something like that."

"That seems kind of fucked up."

He shrugged. "It was their way of softening the blow, I think. Something good to go along with the bad news."

"I guess I can see that." I dried my hands on a dish towel. "What was that like? Being away at sea for months at a time?"

Adam's expression darkened a little. "It was...weird. I did seven deployments, and I still never quite got used to it."

"Really?"

He nodded, resting an elbow on the back of his chair. "Well, I mean, I did seven deployments on four ships, so it was usually on a different ship with a different crew from the last cruise, and we went to different parts of the world." With his free hand, he idly ran a finger around the base of his wineglass. "Tell you one thing, I never got used to being crammed into a tin can with five thousand people and still being lonely."

"Oh my God. I can't even imagine."

"It's part of the navy life." He sighed. "And it's weird, you know? On one hand, you're lonely as fuck. But you know how sometimes when something gets to you, you just want to be alone for a while? Maybe break down, or maybe just sit and catch your breath without anybody else around?"

I nodded. "Yeah, I know that feeling."

Adam swallowed. "There's a certain irony in feeling like you're completely alone out in the middle of the ocean and not being able to find even the smallest little nook to actually *be* alone for a few minutes."

"Wow." I reached for my glass that suddenly didn't have nearly enough wine in it. "I can't even imagine."

He took a long drink, and his own glass was nearly empty now too. I offered the bottle, topped off both our glasses, and we drank in silence for a few minutes.

Then he put his down with a quiet clink. "I could technically stay in for a few more years. See if I make Senior Chief, then maybe stick it out and try for Master Chief. Retire at thirty years instead of twenty and get seventy-five percent retirement pay instead of fifty."

"Sounds like a pretty sweet deal," I said. "Financially, anyway."

"It is, but..." Adam shook his head. "I can't. Honestly, I seriously considered getting out when I reenlisted the last time, but I figured after fourteen years, I might as well suck it up, put in the last six and walk away with a retirement."

"I suppose that makes sense," I said. "But six years is still a long time."

"It's almost over," he said with a shrug. "Down to a few months now."

"Was it worth it?"

"The whole twenty or the last six?"

"Either or. Not like you can change it now, right?"

"True." He looked out the window for a moment, fixing his gaze on the glittering city below us. "I'm just looking forward to having my feet on the same dry land for a while. Maybe even working with the same people for more than a few years."

"Oh, yeah," I said. "I never thought of that. That all the moving around meant you were changing coworkers too."

Adam nodded. "You're never in one command for very long, and everyone else is moving around too. It's constantly a whole different set of faces. It's like starting over every time. You lose touch with people, and..." He blew out a breath. "The next thing you know, you've only got a few people left."

"Wow." I'd been in the same place so long, I couldn't even fathom what it was like to uproot so often.

Adam's eyes lost focus. "Can I tell you something that really made me rethink whether I was cut out for the navy?"

"Sure. Yeah." I took another drink, because I was pretty sure I was going to need it.

"I was on cruise when Jackie and I finally decided to call it quits. My mom was *pissed* because she adored Jackie, and she had it in her head that I'd been cheating or...something. I don't know. But she wasn't thrilled. Anyway, a few days after I got the divorce papers, I got in line for the ship's phones just like I did every Thursday night. You know, to call home. Waited an hour and a half. Finally got to a phone, took out my card, and I..." Adam trailed off.

I resisted the urge to reach out and put a hand over his. "What?"

He met my eyes. "I didn't have anyone to call."

My heart dropped. "No one?"

He shook his head. "No one I could talk to about that, no."

"My God."

He lowered his gaze and watched himself running his thumb back and forth along the edge of the counter. Then he cleared his throat. "Anyway. I didn't mean for that conversation to take such a depressing turn." He laughed halfheartedly. "I asked about you, and now I'm rambling about me. Sorry about that."

"Don't worry about it. Sounds like you've had a difficult career."

"It's been challenging," he said. "And don't get me wrong, I don't regret enlisting. It's been a great career even if it's been tough. I'm just looking forward to retiring from the navy, finding a job and settling down somewhere." He met my eyes again. "It doesn't even matter where right now. I'm just tired of this life."

"I'll bet you are," I said softly.

"And aside from this little depressing segue," he said, "I just want to tell you it's been really great spending time together."

I smiled. "Yeah, it has. Kind of nice to catch up after all this time."

Adam nodded. "It has been. We should do it again."

Damn good thing I wasn't taking a drink just then, or I'd have choked. "Oh. You...you want to get together again?"

"Of course I do." He laughed. "Why wouldn't I?"

"Well, besides the fact that I live in Seattle and you live in San Diego?"

"Airfare's cheap," he said with a dismissive gesture. "Besides, I'm here now. Who's to say we can't do it again?"

"You also had a convenient excuse this time, but what about next time? Are we really going to get together just for the hell of it?"

Adam looked in my eyes. "Do we need a reason?"

"Well, um…" I cleared my throat. "Actually, now that I think about it, a couple of my friends are getting married in a few months. They're doing kind of a bachelor party in Vegas the first weekend of August." I raised my eyebrows. "Want to join us?"

"A bachelor weekend?"

I nodded. "Long story, but one of the grooms is a reformed manwhore, and the other never got a chance to *be* a manwhore."

Adam laughed. "So he's getting one last hurrah? With his fiancé right there?"

I grinned. "It'll make sense when you meet these guys."

"Hell, why not? It sounds like fun."

"Great. I'll send you the dates."

He raised his glass and winked. "I'll be there."

It was still dark, which meant I had no business being conscious. What the hell.

I tossed a few times. Turned a few more times. I was wide awake though, damn it.

I grabbed my phone off the nightstand and turned it on, squinting until my eyes adjusted to the brightness.

4:28.

Sighing, I shut off the phone and set it down before I let my head drop back onto the pillow. I didn't have to be to work until nine, and most days I was lucky to be conscious before seven. What the hell indeed.

Trying to get back to sleep turned out to be an exercise in futility, so I got up, pulled on a pair of boxers and my bathrobe, and then shuffled into the kitchen to put the coffee on. Might as well get up and get caffeinated instead of lying in bed, cursing about being awake.

The first drop of coffee had barely hit the bottom of my cup when, down the hall, a door opened, then closed. My heart kicked into high gear. Adam. Of course he was up. He had to catch the airport shuttle soon. Which meant he was leaving. Fuck.

Fortunately, he decided to grab a shower before he came down the hall. That gave me a few minutes to adjust to the fact that he was awake. And maybe get myself a little worked up about that fact. And the fact that he was leaving.

Well, this was a first. Not quite five in the morning, and I was wide awake enough I really didn't need to bother with coffee. My boss would frown on me wandering into the firm after a bottle or three of wine, though, so I just poured myself a second cup of coffee even though I didn't really need it.

The shower turned off. Movement at the end of the hall. Doors opening and closing. And then footsteps.

Adam stepped into the kitchen in jeans and a T-shirt. His hair was too short to be terribly mussed, but it still had that damp, finger-combed look that I so loved. He looked good. Of course he did. When didn't he?

"You're awake?" he asked.

"Well, it's either that or I'm sleepwalking."

Adam laughed. "You didn't have to get up, you know. No point in both of us being bleary-eyed for the day."

I shrugged as I stirred my already well-stirred coffee. "I usually get up pretty early."

"Bullshit, you do." He chuckled. "I know it's been a long time, but there's no way Dale Ramsey has turned into a morning person."

Heat rushed into my cheeks, and I didn't bother trying to fool him. "Okay, I couldn't sleep."

He raised his eyebrows. "Something bothering you?"

"No, I... it happens sometimes." I waved a hand. "Nothing to worry about. Coffee?"

He eyed me skeptically, but then nodded. "Sure."

I poured him a cup, and we didn't talk for a while. So weird, just standing in my kitchen, me in my pajamas and Adam dressed and ready to go.

"So, um." I tapped my fingers on the counter. "What time does your shuttle get here?"

"I scheduled it for six fifteen."

That soon? Damn it...

He glanced at the clock. "That should give me enough time to get to my gate. Right?"

"Um, it..." I shifted my weight. "When does your flight leave?"

"Nine forty-five."

"You should be fine, then."

"Good, good." He sipped his coffee. "Thanks again, by the way. For putting me up and showing me around town."

"Any time," I said. "Door's always open if you're in town." *It shouldn't be, but we both know it is.*

He smiled. "Thanks."

Maybe ten minutes later, the shuttle arrived. Adam didn't need any help with his bag, since he'd packed fairly light, but I walked him to the door. After the driver had taken his bag, Adam faced me, and my heart didn't know whether to beat like mad because he was this close or drop into my feet because he was about to leave.

"Well." He swallowed. "I guess I'd better go."

I nodded. "Have a safe flight."

"Thanks." Then he reached for me, and he hugged me tight. "It was good to see you."

"You too," I whispered.

As he let me go, he cleared his throat and then smiled. "I'll see you in Vegas?"

"Yeah." I managed to smile too. "See you in Vegas."

We held each other's gazes. Maybe it was the caffeine or the early hour or just my fucked-up brain, but I swore I'd seen that look in his eyes before. Yeah, I had. About three seconds before I realized Adam wasn't as straight as I'd always thought.

I muffled a cough as I broke eye contact, and I gestured at the shuttle. "Guess I shouldn't keep you. Don't want you missing your flight."

"Right. Yeah." He stepped outside. "I'll, um, see you soon."

"Definitely."

And with that, he turned and walked away. As soon as he was in the van, I closed the door and leaned against it. I shut my eyes as I listened to the van's engine fade into the distance.

See you in Vegas.

It dawned on me now that the whole point of that weekend was to be the bachelor party to end all bachelor parties. A group of wild men, a lot of alcohol and whatever Sin City's strip joints and night clubs could throw at us. It would be, to say the least, one hell of a sexually charged weekend.

And I couldn't decide if bringing Adam along was a recipe for disaster or a really fucking good idea.

Guess I'll find out in a few weeks...

Chapter Eight

Considering Alex had never been with any man except Kieran—though I had my suspicions about what sometimes happened between them and Ethan and Rhett—it was only fair we should all take him to Las Vegas before he got married. Everyone deserved a little sin and debauchery in their lives, especially someone with such an oppressive history. The wedding wasn't for a few months yet, but since Alex was on summer break from college, it was the perfect time for a trip to Sin City.

It was also the perfect opportunity for another "as long as we're in the same general area" visit with Adam. Okay, so Vegas was like five hours by car from San Diego, but whatever. Adam took a short hop and agreed to meet me in the lobby of one of the casinos so we could grab dinner before we joined the guys. We'd have met outside, but it was just too fucking hot. August? In the desert? Fuck that.

In the air-conditioned lobby, slot machines clanked and beeped. There was a steady murmur of voices, punctuated by the occasional shout of glee—usually followed by the beeps and sirens of a winning slot machine—or drunken laugh.

I scanned the thick crowd of anonymous faces. He'd texted me earlier to say his plane had landed, but I was still irrationally afraid he'd thought better of this whole thing and wasn't coming. After all, we were tempting fate by meeting up in this city for a bachelor party with those four dirty bastards. Well, six. Kieran's ex, Sebastian, would be there with his new boyfriend, and though I'd only met those two a couple of times, it was a safe bet they weren't a couple of uptight prudes.

Prolonged exposure to Kieran seemed to cure most people of that.

Anyway. The six of them plus the two of us. Adam didn't know any of them from, well, Adam, but a bachelor party in Las Vegas always meant sin, debauchery and, of course, temptation. Who was I to judge him if he decided that temptation was too—

There.

There he was.

In spite of my nerves, I couldn't help smiling. After so many years apart, the novelty of seeing him in person definitely hadn't worn off. I was really starting to like this not-quite-silver-but-close fox look, too. He was hot when he was younger, but he wore his late thirties well enough, I imagined he was going to rival Ethan for making the forties his bitch.

"Hey," he said with a grin when he was close enough to hear over the casino's noise. "Hope I'm not late."

I shook my head. "Don't worry about it. This is going to be one long night, so a few minutes won't make much difference." I glanced at my watch. "In fact, we've got plenty of time before we need to go join up with them."

Adam grinned. "Can't wait."

"Should we get something to eat first?"

"Absolutely."

We left the casino and headed out onto the Strip in search of something that wasn't ridiculously expensive and wasn't a buffet.

"So have you ever been to Vegas?" I asked as we walked down the crowded sidewalk.

"I, um..." His cheeks colored.

"What?" I paused, then snorted. "You got married here, didn't you?"

Laughing, he nodded. "Only once, though."

"Oh. Well. That changes everything."

"Was that sarcasm?"

"Of course it was." I slid my hands into the pockets of my shorts—it was fucking hot, sue me—and scanned some of the signs, still looking for a halfway decent place to eat. "So which time was that?"

"Which time was what?"

I turned toward him. "I mean, when you got married here. First, second or third time around?"

"First."

"Seriously?"

He shrugged. "Why not?"

"I don't know, I guess I just figured..." Trailing off, I shook my head. "I don't know. I don't know what I thought."

"We were being young, stupid and impulsive," Adam said. "And we were doing it on short notice so we could make sure we got the same orders." He waved a hand at the glittering lights of the Strip. "So, Vegas it was."

"Okay, I guess that makes sense." In a way, I supposed it did, but I still couldn't get my head around Adam even being married, never mind running off to Vegas for a quickie under a neon sign with an Elvis impersonator for a minister. That just wasn't...him. I thought, anyway.

"Come on," he said. "You can't really be that surprised. I seem to recall you witnessed plenty of my stupidity when it came to women."

"True," I said, snickering. "But that was high school."

"And some of us need a few years after high school to grow up." He glanced at me. "Hey, you remember when Katie Dixon dumped me our junior year?"

I laughed aloud. "Oh God, yes."

"I'll never forget you offering to kick her ass for me."

"Yeah, well, I'm kind of glad you didn't take me up on it." I grimaced. "A varsity wrestler against a choir boy? That could've gotten ugly."

Adam laughed. "She'd have broken you in half."

"And I was *still* willing to take her on for breaking your heart." I wagged a finger at him. "That's some best-friend dedication, right there."

"Okay, okay, I won't argue with that." We slipped past a crowd of tourists watching a street mime, and then Adam said, "And as long as we're on the subject of high school, I've been wondering this for years: What the fuck did you ever see in Ricky Slater?"

I smothered a laugh. "Well, you never saw him with his pants off."

Adam's jaw dropped. "You actually fucked him?"

"Uh, yeah." I looked at him like he'd lost his mind. "What did you think we were doing? Sitting in his parents' living room reading fairy tales to each other?"

"I, well..." He cleared his throat. "I guess I didn't give it a lot of...a lot of thought."

I looked at him and furrowed my brow. His eyes flicked toward me, but he quickly looked straight ahead. Part of me wanted to pursue that topic and find out just what he'd thought back then—did he think of me? Did he think of any guys? Did he know he was gay or bi or whatever by then?—but that had the potential to turn this evening into an awkward one, so as we continued past the entrance to another casino, I changed the subject.

"Remember when we wrapped Mr. Langley's car in bubble wrap?" I snickered. "I don't think his bald spot ever turned redder than it did that day."

Adam laughed. "Man, I thought we were dead meat over that."

"Me too. Hey, how were we supposed to know it was hot enough to melt the plastic onto the paint?"

"Still, I thought we were *fucked* over that."

"You and me both."

We stopped to wait for a crosswalk signal to change. While we waited, he said, "It's funny, isn't it? High school seemed so important back then. Like everything was earth-shattering and life-altering. A failed test was going to follow you around for the rest of your life."

"Or that two weeks of detention was going to come up in a job interview at NASA, and you'd end up being a janitor at the DMV."

"Or a failed relationship would mean you were doomed to be alone forever."

Our eyes met. My breath caught. So did his.

I broke eye contact first, clearing my throat because that *so* didn't add to the awkwardness of the moment. "So, um. Any restaurants sound good?"

He took a breath like he was about to say something, but let it go. Nodding, he gestured at a Greek-looking restaurant across the street. "That one looks like it's worth a try."

"We'll give it a go, then." I forced a laugh. "Can't be any worse than ship food, right?"

His laugh was a little more genuine. "Well, just don't expect me to order the steak and lobster."

When the light turned green, we crossed the street and went inside, and, thank God, kept the conversation light. We weren't here to revisit our awkward past. We were here to have a good time, and damn it, that was exactly what we were going to do.

At a little before eight, we walked into the club where the guys had said to meet them.

"So how many of us are going to be here?" Adam asked.

"Eight, I think." I ran the names through my head. "Yeah, eight." I nodded toward the booth in the corner where everyone was already working their way through some cocktails. "And there they are."

"Hey, about time you showed up!" Kieran said, gesturing at us with his glass.

"Yeah, yeah," I said. "Just being fashionably late. You know me. Anyway, Adam, this is Rhett and his husband Ethan."

Ethan scowled. "Why am I always the husband? Why is it never Ethan and *his* husband Rhett?"

I rolled my eyes. "Because you're Rhett's bitch and everybody knows it. Now hush."

Rhett smothered a laugh. So did Adam.

I introduced him to Sebastian and Luke, and of course, Kieran and Alex. Adam shook hands with each in turn.

"Alex is Kieran's fiancé," I explained. "He's the reason we're all here to have some fun."

"Congratulations," Adam said to Alex and Kieran. "Don't think I've ever been to a bachelor party where both grooms came along."

Alex put an arm around Kieran's shoulders. "You obviously underestimate how much of a bad influence my groom is on me." He glanced at his fiancé and smirked. "A bachelor party wouldn't be nearly as fun and insane without him."

"Damn right it wouldn't." Kieran kissed Alex.

"All right, all right," Luke said. "Get a room, you two."

"Now let's not be hasty," I said. "Are we all going to this room with them or what?"

All the guys laughed, and they shuffled around to make room for us in the booth.

"Damn it, I need a refill." Ethan gestured with his empty glass. "Anyone else?"

Everyone put a hand up.

Ethan gave an exasperated sigh. "How the hell am I supposed to carry that much?"

"We still need to get drinks anyway, so I'll help," Adam said with a laugh, and got up.

"Thanks," Ethan said. "At least *someone's* willing to give me a hand."

As Adam followed Ethan across the lounge toward the bar, Rhett and Alex both craned their necks, making no small gesture of watching Adam.

"*Alex,*" Kieran scolded playfully. "What have I told you about scoping out other men's asses?"

Alex batted his eyes in a flawless display of innocence. "Do it as often as possible?"

"Mm-hmm. And?"

"And—" Alex's expression turned sheepish. "Point him out to you so you can gawk too."

"Exactly." Kieran patted his leg. "You're learning."

"To be fair, he was sitting with us." Alex gestured at Adam's empty seat. "And he walked right past you on his way out. So I naturally assumed you'd gotten an eyeful right then."

"And what happens when you assume?"

"You miss out on a gorgeous ass because you need to get glasses?"

The rest of us laughed. Kieran just rolled his eyes.

"I have to give you credit, Dale," Rhett said. "He is *hot.*"

"Isn't he?"

Kieran smirked. "Isn't he a little young for you, Rhett?"

"Shut up." Rhett threw a peanut, which bounced off Kieran's forehead.

"He's older than you, isn't he?" Alex said.

"Quiet, you," Kieran muttered.

"Yeah," I said. "The grownups are talking."

"Oh, fuck you both."

Rhett leaned in closer and lowered his voice. "So what's the deal with you two, anyway? You said you were just friends, but he's here, and...?" His raised eyebrow finished the question.

"Well, he lives in San Diego, and Vegas is kind of a...um... It's sort of a halfway point. Seemed like we might as well meet up while I was here."

"Meet up?" Rhett asked. "Or hook up?"

Don't I wish?

"We're just friends," I said. "But we don't see each other often. So this seemed like a good opportunity."

"Mm-hmm." Kieran gave me the same upraised-eyebrow look that Rhett did.

"So let me get this straight," Rhett said. "You guys are just friends, but you've hooked up before, and now you're here? Together? And you're not planning to hook up with him?"

I reached for my drink. "When you put it like that, it suddenly sounds insane."

He shrugged. "I'm just wondering if you're tempting fate— and yourselves—by getting together in this kind of setting."

I didn't answer. Just took a drink. A really long drink.

"So what about Owen?" Kieran asked. "You called him yet?"

"I, um..." I set my glass down. "I haven't."

He elbowed me. "Come on, man. Guy like that's not going to stay on the market very long. Trust me."

I glanced at the bar to make sure Ethan and Adam were still occupied. "Why? You know something I don't?"

"I know the deejay at Wilde's has been giving him the I-wanna-piece-of-that look for the last week or two." He nudged my arm again. "You want a shot at him? I'd suggest you get on the ball." He inclined his head. "Unless you have someone else on your list?" His eyes flicked toward Adam, then back to me.

Oh hell. What did I have to lose? I wasn't here "with" Adam. Maybe setting something up with another guy was just what I needed to remind myself of that.

"All right." I pulled out my phone. "I'll text him and see if he's free."

"That's the spirit," Kieran said.

I pulled up Owen's number and typed, *It's Dale again—want to meet for drinks this week?*

And without a second's hesitation, sent.

"There." I set the phone facedown on the table. "Done."

Rhett didn't flash me a smug look or anything, but a slightly puzzled one.

Kieran clapped me on the shoulder. "Let me know how it goes." He winked. "I want all the details if you score with that one."

"*Kieran,*" Alex said.

"What?"

I just laughed, and right then, Adam and Ethan returned with drinks for all of us. Sebastian and Rhett took some of the glasses from their arms to keep any of them from dropping.

"You know," I said, "they do have servers in places like this."

"Not this joint," Ethan muttered. "Unless we want to wait all damned night."

Rhett laughed. "Yeah, but if we let you carry all those drinks, you're going to end up wearing them."

"No big deal," Luke said with a shrug. "We can just tell people we were doing body shots off him."

Ethan raised an eyebrow as he slid into the booth beside Rhett. "Doing what now?"

"Yeah." Luke cocked his head. "You do know what body shots are, don't you?"

"Uh, no."

Kieran's jaw dropped. "You've never done body shots before?"

Ethan shook his head. "No, I have a feeling it was before their time."

Laughing, Kieran nodded. "Yeah, I suspect you're right."

"Well," Sebastian said. "This *is* a bachelor party. Body shots, anyone?"

"I'm game." Kieran looked at Alex, who shrugged, and then Kieran rubbed his hands together. "I nominate Alex for the body, and now all we need is some salt, lime, and—"

"Uh, Kieran?" Rhett put a hand on his arm. "You *do* remember what tequila does to Ethan, right?"

Kieran flashed a broad grin. "You're damn right I do."

Rhett laughed and sat back, shaking his head and putting his arm around Ethan as Kieran got up from the booth. We all watched as he went to the bar and flagged down the bartender. He leaned across the bar and whispered something, and the bartender grinned, then nodded.

"Looks like we're doing body shots," I said.

"Um." Ethan gave us each a slightly wary look. "Is someone going to explain what these are before I agree to them?"

"Nope." Rhett patted his arm. "Just watch. You'll catch on."

Ethan raised his eyebrows. "Don't tell me you've done these."

"I haven't done them, but I know what they are." Rhett kissed Ethan's cheek. "It'll be fun. Trust me."

I turned to Adam. "You ever done body shots?"

Adam just grinned, and I shivered.

Then he leaned toward me. "So, um, out of curiosity, what exactly does tequila do to Ethan? He doesn't get stupid, does he?"

"Nope. Tequila in him is like Extasy in the rest of us."

Adam's eyes widened. He glanced at Ethan and chuckled. "This I gotta see."

A moment later, Kieran came back to the booth. "Bartender said they don't usually allow body shots because it can get a little out of hand, but it's still early"—he grinned—"so we can use the VIP lounge since it's empty."

Ethan gave Rhett a slightly alarmed look, and Rhett and I both smothered laughs. Oh, if he only knew what he was getting himself into.

Though as I followed the other guys out of the booth and into the VIP lounge, my stomach fluttered with nerves. We were going into a private room for body shots off a hot guy. There'd be drinking. There'd be mouths on skin.

And there'd be Adam.

You knew things would get racy when you invited him, some voice in my head reminded me. *Isn't that why you invited him?*

No, of course it wasn't.

Friends, right? Being in an alcohol-saturated and sexually charged atmosphere didn't change that. Did it?

I glanced at Adam as he and Ethan shared a laugh over something, and goose bumps rose under my shirt. *Ooh,* no. The atmosphere didn't change a goddamned thing, except maybe shining a spotlight on the fact that I wanted Adam between the sheets of my hotel bed.

Maybe this was a good opportunity to prove to myself we could be just friends without anything happening or getting awkward. I was physically attracted to every other man in this group, and could be around them even in the most sexually charged situations without losing my head, so that meant I was perfectly capable of doing that with Adam. Tonight, I'd prove that.

The VIP lounge had a couple of booths and a long table, which Kieran and Rhett moved to the center of the small room. They tested it, making sure it was sturdy and stable, and it looked like it would hold up.

"So, um." Alex looked at Kieran, lifting his eyebrows. "How does this work?"

"You take off your shirt and lay on the table." He winked. "We'll handle the rest."

"I like the sound of that." Alex took off his shirt. Wasn't the first time I'd seen him without it, but that kid's physique was breathtaking. And that six-pack was suspiciously better defined than the last time I'd seen him topless, so I had a feeling Rhett and Kieran had taught him a thing or two in Ethan and Rhett's home gym.

He lay back across the table.

The bartender came in with the necessities: a shaker of salt, a bowl of lime wedges, and of course, a bottle of Cuervo. Kieran slipped him a folded-up bill and a flirtatious grin and whispered something to him that I couldn't hear. The bartender hesitated but finally returned the grin and handed over the bottle of tequila.

Kieran stood next to the table and held up the bottle. "Ready?"

Alex put his hands behind his head, which only pulled his abs that much tighter. "Whenever you are."

Kieran tilted the bottle above the groove at the apex of Alex's ab muscles, right between his pecs. He let a single drop of clear liquid fall, and as soon as it touched the divot in Alex's chest, Alex gasped and his back arched off the table. As he settled back down, probably once the shock of the cold wore off, Kieran poured some more, leaving a small pool on Alex's skin.

Rhett handed Alex a lime wedge. "Hold it between your teeth."

Alex put it in his mouth, peel-in, and again rested his hands behind his head. He grinned around the lime wedge at Kieran.

Kieran returned it. Then he looked at us. "Anyone object to me going first?"

"I think the groom should have first crack at, well, the groom." Rhett gestured at Alex. "Have at him, Kieran."

"With pleasure." Kieran leaned down, and closed his mouth over the pool of tequila. Alex bit his lip and shivered. I was pretty sure every one of us had the exact same reaction, and I doubted there was a man in the room who didn't get goose bumps when Kieran ran his tongue up the thin line of salt and then bit the lime wedge in Alex's mouth.

Kieran took the wedge out of his own mouth, and the two of them exchanged grins before he leaned down and kissed Alex.

Then he stood and looked at the rest of us. "Any questions, Ethan?"

Ethan exhaled hard and shook his head. "Nope. Think I got it."

"Well, just to be sure." Rhett gently nudged Ethan out of the way. "Maybe you should watch one more time."

"Hey!" But then Ethan glanced at Alex, Rhett, Alex again, and shrugged. "Okay, yeah, I'm good with watching this."

"Thought so." Rhett winked at Ethan.

Kieran poured the tequila and sprinkled the salt. Alex's abs quivered as Rhett slowly licked away the tequila. A moment later, Rhett's piercing glinted in the light as he drew the tip of his tongue up the middle of Alex's chest. Then the lime wedge disappeared between their mouths, and I wondered if either of them even tasted the lime with the way they were kissing.

Well. I'd wondered for a while now if Kieran had introduced Alex to Rhett and Ethan's bedroom. Watching them draw out a kiss like that? Mystery solved.

Rhett stood, then took a seat beside Adam and me as Ethan moved in for his turn with Alex. If I'd ever had any reason to question what Kieran saw in Alex—and I hadn't—that swell beneath his belt would've convinced me. And air-conditioning be damned, it was getting *hot* in here.

I squirmed in my seat. "Just how much have you corrupted that poor lad, Kieran?"

"Poor lad?" Adam laughed. "He doesn't look too 'poor' to me."

"Hey," Kieran said. "I've merely done my duty as a manwhore and taught him to enjoy the...finer things in life."

I eyed Kieran. "Having Ethan lick tequila off his chest and take a lime wedge out of his mouth qualifies as one of the finer things in life?"

We all watched as Ethan took the lime wedge from his own mouth before he leaned down and, just like Rhett did before, kissed Alex full-on.

In unison, we all said, "Yeah. It does."

Sebastian took his turn. Luke hesitated, but Sebastian encouraged him, so he did too. Alex was getting more than a little flustered, his cheeks flushed and his cock obviously hard, and Kieran wasn't helping, whispering things in his ear and kissing him in between pouring tequila for the rest of us.

When it was Adam's turn, he got up and whispered something to Kieran, and, judging by Kieran's grin, it had to be something dirty and mischievous.

"Good idea," Kieran said. "Guys, we're changing the rules a little." He licked his finger, and then drew a line up the side of Alex's throat, making Alex squirm and tilt his head to one side. Kieran sprinkled some salt on that invisible line, and Jesus H. Christ, I swore the air conditioning had crapped out completely. It was hot as hell in this room now.

As Kieran picked up the bottle of tequila, he looked at Adam. "Ready?"

"Definitely."

Kieran gave Alex another lime wedge, and then poured the tequila in that divot on his chest.

Adam put a hand on the table beside Alex's chest, and as he leaned down, both jealousy and arousal simultaneously tightened my throat. My stomach muscles contracted just thinking about Adam licking tequila off my chest, and I couldn't breathe at all as Adam made a slow, sensuous gesture of taking the salt off Alex's neck.

When he went for the lime wedge, he bit it just right to keep from touching Alex's lips with his own, but Alex grabbed the back of his neck and made sure he got a kiss from Adam just like he did from everyone else.

And I was the one who was out of breath. Holy *fuck*.

Then Adam looked at me, and that grin threatened to melt my knees right out from under me. "I think it's your turn, isn't it?"

I cleared my throat. "I, um, I guess it is."

Kieran held up the salt shaker. "You want it on his neck or his chest?"

"I vote neck," Alex said just before he put another lime wedge between his teeth.

"The groom has spoken," I said with as much of a laugh as my constricting throat would allow. "On the neck."

Salt was sprinkled. Tequila was poured. The lime wedge was ready. Was I? Only one way to find out.

I balanced myself with a hand on the edge of the table and leaned down. The tequila made my eyes water, and Alex's body heat certainly didn't help. As I licked the salt off his neck, I shivered, resisting the urge to glance at Adam and see if he was watching. If he was as enthralled as I'd been when he'd done this a moment ago.

I hesitated before taking the lime from Alex. "Do I get to kiss you too?"

His eyebrows wiggled, and when I leaned down, sure enough, he kissed me. The lime was tart, and the combination of salt, tequila, and lime had my senses swirling already, but as soon as I'd moved the wedge out of the way with my tongue, it was Alex's kiss that really had me spinning. Gone was the shy kid who'd hooked up with Kieran a while back; he kissed like he knew what he wanted and he'd be damned if anyone stopped him from getting it. As if he hadn't been hot enough already.

I broke the kiss, exchanged a quick look with him, and stood, chewing the piece of lime I'd kept tucked into my cheek.

And yes, Adam was watching.

He gulped, shifting in his chair. I didn't dare let myself look to see if his shorts were fitting any tighter. The smoldering look in his eyes was more than enough to tell me he was turned on.

We can't go there, that damned voice in the back of my mind whispered. *We agreed. Just friends. Don't fuck this up over some sex and tequila.*

I broke eye contact and turned away as I took the lime rind out of my mouth. We wouldn't screw this up. We could be here and in this sexy environment, and walk away as friends just like every man in this room could. We could, and we would, damn it.

Alex sat up, brushing a few grains of salt off his neck and chest. "Well. Now that we're all warmed up, didn't someone say something about going to a strip club?"

Thankful for the diversion, I said, "A strip club sounds good to me."

"Good." Rhett handed Alex his shirt. "Because we know just the place."

Chapter Nine

Three clubs, a few dozen lap dances and God knows how much booze later, a cab dropped Adam and me in front of our hotel. Neither of us was all that drunk by this point, though. A little buzzed, and we'd probably both be hating life tomorrow, but we'd stopped drinking a couple of hours ago when the tab crept up on entirely too much money.

As we walked from the cab to the hotel, I tugged at my collar. "Jesus. I thought the desert was supposed to get cold at night."

"It *is* August."

"Hmm, yeah. Good point."

Adam yawned. "Man, I think I'm getting too old for this."

"Tell me about it. Christ, when did we *get* old, anyway?"

"I don't know. Kind of snuck up on us."

"Man. Next thing I know, I'm going to wake up and be Ethan's age."

Adam laughed. "Yeah, and how the hell does he keep up with everyone else? He looked like he had a few hours left in him."

"Oh God. I don't know. I think he sold his soul or something. Hell, I'd sell mine to look that good in my forties."

"Maybe his penance is hanging around a bunch of younger guys who rib him about his age at every opportunity."

"Penance?" I snorted. "He licked salt off Alex's bare abs, and God knows what the four of them are going to get up to now that they're unsupervised. If that's what you call penance, sign me up."

Adam nodded. "Agreed."

We walked into the hotel lobby, which was just as loud and crowded at five in the morning as it had been in the evening. We didn't talk, we just dragged ourselves to the elevator and pushed the buttons for our respective floors.

As the elevator rose, Adam said, "Want to hit up the buffet for breakfast in the morning?"

I rubbed my eyes. "Probably more like lunch at this rate."

He laughed quietly. "I feel that. Text me when you're up if you want to grab something."

"Will do."

My floor was first, so when the elevator stopped, I murmured a good night and then stepped out.

In my room, I shut the door behind me and then toed off my shoes. As soon as I saw the bed, exhaustion wrapped itself around me like a thick, wet blanket, and I shuffled across the carpet, unbuttoning my shirt as I did.

I sat on the bed to finish undressing.

Fatigue set in even harder.

So, still mostly dressed, I lay back across the bed, and that was all she wrote.

When I woke up a few hours later, I shouldn't have been surprised I was alone. I knew full well we'd gone our separate ways before we were anywhere near my room.

Every dream I'd had, though, begged to differ. We'd done body shots off each other. The body shots with the guys had turned into a naked free-for-all... and I'd only touched Adam. We'd skipped the strip clubs and gotten a room, and—

My phone buzzed on the bedside table, sending my heart into my throat. What if he wanted to get breakfast or something before we both headed to our respective homes? What if—

It was a text, but it wasn't from Adam.

Owen

I opened the message.

I have Tuesday night off. Drinks?

I exhaled.

Last night was still pounding too hard on the inside of my skull for me to even want to think about going out in the near future, but I also needed to drive the point home to myself that I wasn't hung up on Adam. I was not. I refused to be. Yeah, we were attracted to each other, but we'd made it through last night without doing anything we shouldn't have, so we could do this.

And I could do this, so I texted Owen back, *Tuesday evening sounds great.*

Okay, so it didn't sound great. But by Tuesday afternoon, it would, so fuck it.

After I'd showered and dressed, I texted Adam to see if he wanted to get breakfast. Or brunch. Hell, this late in the day, it was lunch. He did, so I joined him downstairs and we walked to the Bellagio, since rumor had it there was a buffet near that casino that was excellent.

After lunch, which lived up to its hype, we strolled outside.

"By the way," I said as we walked by the Bellagio's massive fountain, "it was good to see you again."

Adam smiled at me, and I tried not to read too much into the fact that his eyes looked a little sad. He was just tired. Probably hung over. That was all. "Too bad we don't live closer."

"Yeah, true."

We stopped for a moment to watch the fountain, but something about the silence between us was loaded. Like we'd only stopped so one of us could collect his thoughts and maybe put them into words. I didn't want to ruin this with something awkward and didn't dare let myself imagine that anything we wanted to say would be anything but awkward, so I struggled to find an easy, light topic to carry us until we went our separate ways.

But Adam spoke first.

"By the way, what we were talking about last night? About things from high school turning out to be meaningless?" He turned his head toward me. "I didn't mean us."

"I knew what you meant. We didn't have a relationship."

"No, but we—"

"Adam." I faced him fully, and he mirrored me. "It was high school. It's in the past. We're friends again. Let's not overanalyze it."

"I don't want to overanalyze it," he said. "I just didn't want you to think that night... I mean, we were kids, and we both still had a lot of growing up to do, and..." He paused, exhaling sharply as he looked toward the fountain again. "I don't even know what I'm trying to say."

"If it helps, I know you weren't talking about us last night."

Liar, liar...

He still didn't look at me.

I shifted my weight, sliding my hands into my pockets. "I don't think—"

"Do you ever wonder what would've happened if we'd both stayed in Orlando?" he asked suddenly.

"We'd, um, we'd have very different careers now."

"You know what I mean."

"Adam." I pushed out a breath. "Don't. Please. I don't want to go there." *Not unless you want to go all the way there, and let's not kid ourselves.*

Our eyes met. The soft rippling reflection from the fountain played on the side of his face and in his eyes. I could have sworn we'd been standing farther apart, but he was unnervingly close now. I imagined him reaching for me, and in spite of the desert heat, my skin felt cool in all the places my mind's eye could see him touching me. A hand on my waist, the other on my face, his chest against mine, his hips against mine; I barely kept myself from shivering.

"Dale..." He shifted a little, still holding my gaze. His lips were apart, like he still intended to say something, but then his eyes flicked toward my lips.

I gulped.

Our eyes met again.

Kiss me. For the love of all that's holy, man, kiss me.

He bit his lip.

Stay back. For the sake of this friendship and my sanity, stay back.

He swallowed, and I couldn't help glancing at his throat as his Adam's apple jumped.

Kiss me.

Stay back.

An image flickered through my mind of Adam licking salt off Alex's neck just before—

Kiss me.

Stay with me tonight.

I muffled a cough and turned away. "We should, um, head back. If we're going to get to the airport before our flights leave."

"Right. Yeah. Good idea."

We looked at each other again, and though neither of us moved, the narrow space between us seemed to be widening. That realization wasn't the relief it should have been.

"Anyway. Um." He gestured toward our hotel. "After you?"

I said nothing. Neither did he. Breaking eye contact, we turned and walked back to our hotel.

It wasn't until the elevator stopped at my floor that Adam broke the silence. "It was good seeing you again."

"You too."

And damn him, he hugged me. I closed my eyes, holding on to him for a second or two longer than I probably should have.

He let me go and started to speak, but hesitated. "We should do it again. Maybe not, um, here, but—"

"I know what you mean." I chuckled. "Maybe someplace a little tamer?"

"Yeah. That."

The elevator doors started closing, and Adam caught them.

"I'd better go," I said. "Talk to you on the webcam?"

He smiled. "Absolutely."

I stepped out of the elevator, and we held each other's gazes until the doors closed again, and then I headed for my room.

Sitting on the edge of the bed, I rubbed my temples. This weekend had been exhausting, but it was fun, and now it was over. Somehow, Adam and I hadn't crossed any lines. Blurred a few, maybe, but we hadn't crossed them. I just couldn't decide if I was relieved or disappointed.

But it didn't matter. My flight left in a few hours, and Adam was on his way back to San Diego too. We were on our way back to our own lives. We were still just friends.

And on Tuesday night, I had a date with Owen.

Chapter Ten

Tuesday showed up fucking quick. I was still shaking off a little fatigue from Vegas—what was it about that city that made us think we could stay up until all hours of the night?—as I stood in my bedroom getting ready for my date with Owen.

Fatigue aside, why did I feel so weird about this? About going on a date when I was still catching my breath from a weekend with Adam? That weekend hadn't just been with him, anyway. And even if it was, it wasn't like I was cheating on him tonight.

As I changed my shirt for the eleventh time, I glanced at my phone, which sat on the bed next to my wallet. Maybe it was the fact that I hadn't told him what was bothering me. The feeling that even though I didn't need to, I was hiding this from him.

So I picked up the phone.

Won't be on tonight, I wrote in a text. *Got a date.* There. At least now I was being upfront. I didn't owe him the truth, and I didn't need his permission, but telling him took some weight off my shoulders.

A few minutes later, as I was double-checking that I looked like a man who had any business being on a date with a Wilde's bartender, my phone buzzed. A queasy feeling lurched in my gut. What if he was upset? Jealous? Hurt?

So what if he was?

I shook my head and then opened the new message.

Do you? That's great. Good luck. ;)

I smiled to myself, if a little halfheartedly, and sent back, *Thanks. We'll see how it goes.*

Indeed, we would.

I finally settled on something to wear. That was unusual in and of itself; I didn't own a piece of clothing I'd be reluctant to wear, but I was nervous, and worrying about wearing "the wrong thing" was as good a thing as any to channel that nervousness. But I refused to be late on a first date, so I finally got it together and left.

The restaurant wasn't far from where I lived. Such was one of the advantages of living so close to Broadway: anything worth going to was only a few blocks away. The night was warm, if a little damp from some rain this afternoon, so the walk was pleasant.

I was early and didn't see anyone resembling Owen, so I figured he wasn't here yet. I took a seat at the bar and kept an eye on the door.

And right on time—*ooh, that's a plus for you, darling*—he came strolling in through the front door, and I nearly choked on my drink. His pictures hadn't begun to do him justice. The man was six scoops of gorgeous covered with perfect and smothered in "fuck me."

Something told me this date was going to end very, very well.

He walked right up to me and smiled. "Dale?"

"Owen?"

The smile broadened. "That's me." Oh Lord, he really did have a Southern accent.

I stood, and we shook hands. "It's nice to finally meet you."

"You too."

"I'm sorry it took me so long. I've been"—*Hung up on someone else. Pining after the one that got away. Wishing I could be with*—"busy as hell at work."

"Understood," he said. "I've been pulling doubles at the club lately. Great for the wallet, not so much for the knees or the social life."

I laughed. "I'm sure."

The waiter finally made his way down to us and took Owen's drink order.

Once Owen had his drink in hand and had taken a sip, he asked. "So how do you know Kieran?"

"Oh, I"—*know the guys he was fucking when he first moved here a few years ago?*—"met him through a friend of a friend."

Owen nodded. "He's a good guy. Definitely works his ass off at the club."

"As long as he doesn't work that gorgeous ass all the way off."

Owen raised his glass. "Agreed."

Well, that was a plus. He didn't get jealous over me complimenting Kieran's ass. Point in his favor. Though to be fair, who *wouldn't* have complimented that butt? It wasn't something to get jealous over. It was just a goddamned fact.

"So is bartending your thing?" I asked. "Or are you going to school, working toward something else, or...?"

"I used to be an engineer, believe it or not."

"Really?"

He nodded. "Got laid off after five years at Boeing and started bartending to make ends meet while I found something else."

"How long ago was that?"

"Almost three years now." He shrugged and reached for his glass. "I'm not making quite as much money, but you know, I think I'll keep doing this."

"Why's that?"

"Less stress. Not having to deal with the traffic in and out of the plant, not to mention the *hours*." He groaned. "Getting up at three thirty in the morning is inhumane."

"Oh my God." I wrinkled my nose. "I wouldn't last a week."

"You have no idea. It's also kind of nice being able to be completely out. I mean, you can't exactly pretend to be straight at Wilde's, right?"

I laughed. "No, I think just walking in there qualifies any man as being gay."

Owen nodded. "Exactly. And people knew at my old job, but I still felt like I had to keep a lid on it. Couldn't talk about dating anyone. God forbid I compliment someone's shoes. I think the pink slip saved me from getting an ulcer eventually."

"I don't doubt that. So you're just going to keep bartending, then?"

"As long as it pays the bills, why not?"

"Here, here."

"What about you?" he asked. "Kieran said you worked for an architect or something?"

I nodded. "I'm a drafter. I thought about becoming an architect myself, but I actually enjoyed the drafting aspect more than anything, so..." I shrugged. "Here I am."

"So I see." He laughed and shook his head.

"What?" I asked.

"Look at us." He grinned, gesturing with his glass. "Two flaming gay men in a swanky bar in the gayest part of Seattle, and I don't think anyone walking through that door would guess we're really just a couple of nerds."

I threw my head back and laughed. "That's very true. We don't look the part, do we?"

"No." He stroked his chin thoughtfully. "Which begs the question. Are we two gay men being stealthy nerds? Or two nerds being stealthy gay men?"

"Oh, please." I waved a hand. "There is nothing stealthy about me and gay. My nerd side may be as big a secret as Batman, but this Bruce Wayne is *all* the way out of the Bat Cave."

Owen laughed and then drawled, "I think we're gonna get along just fine."

"I think you're right," I said.

After a lovely dinner and some drinks, we left the restaurant. And there we looked at each other in true how-about-a-goodnight-kiss fashion, leaning in close with eyes narrowed, silently daring one another to make The Move.

"I had a great time tonight," Owen said, following the perfect-first-date script to the letter.

"Me too." The response was automatic, and though I meant it, I didn't *mean* it. I'd enjoyed the evening, but not in the flying high, let's-see-where-the-night-takes-us way I should have felt after a great first date.

And we followed the steps as well as the script: look in each other's eyes. Step a little closer. Lift the chin. Tilt the head. Press his lips to mine.

And I felt absolutely nothing. Not a flutter in my chest, not a stir below the belt.

When he drew back and our eyes met again, I still didn't feel a damned thing.

As my hand slid off his arm, I said, "So, um, I'll text you sometime?"

His smile should've made my heart race, and I should have felt a hopeful warmth when he said, "Sure."

Nothing. At all.

Walking home alone from the restaurant, I couldn't make heads or tails of how I felt about this evening. About Owen. First dates were usually either fireworks and fuck-me looks, or I was bored out of my skull and looking for the nearest exit. Sometimes there was just no chemistry, but it was an enjoyable evening anyway. Once in a while, he was a colossal douche bag who I wanted to drown in the soup du jour.

Tonight was none of the above. Owen was a nice guy. Very attractive, obviously intelligent and certainly interesting. Conversation came easy. Sex probably would have too if the thought hadn't made me doubly aware of how much I didn't feel this evening. My God, a gloriously gorgeous man with a brain and a Southern accent had kissed me, and there hadn't been even the slightest stir south of my belt.

Maybe I just wasn't in the mood tonight. I didn't know. I was still a little tired from the trip to Vegas. Sweet Jesus, I really was getting old.

But even if I'd been jetlagged off my ass and hadn't slept in days, good company could usually shake some enthusiasm out of me, and Owen was definitely good company. And a good kisser, for that matter.

After I'd let myself into my condo, I closed the door and tossed my keys onto the table beside it.

The clock above the microwave said it was a little after ten o'clock. What the fuck? I'd been on a date tonight. With a hot, Southern-accented Wilde's bartender. Why the hell was I home at ten seventeen? More to the point, why was I not having sex right now?

Or, even *more* to the point, why the hell didn't I *want* to be having sex right now? What in the name of God was wrong with me?

I didn't even feel like having a glass of wine. Just the thought of going through the motions made me tired, and the alcohol would have me dozing off before too long. Might as well just check my e-mail and call it a night.

I sat on the couch and picked up my computer off the coffee table. Not two minutes after I logged on, a notification popped up:

AdamO wants to chat.

The webcam icon blinked next to it.

Hell, why not? I was tired as hell, but a few minutes of face time wouldn't hurt, so I accepted the request.

A moment later, his face appeared on the screen, and my heart fluttered, and I suddenly wasn't so tired anymore. All evening, I'd felt like I was running at half power, but now all eight cylinders were definitely firing.

"Hey," I said.

"Hey." He smiled. "I thought you were out for the evening."

"Yeah, I..." I shrugged. "Decided not to stay out too late."

He furrowed his brow. "Didn't go well?"

"Oh, it went fine. But I didn't..." I shrugged again, with less enthusiasm this time. "I didn't want to rush things, you know?"

"That's true," he said softly. "Guess it never hurts to take things slow."

We locked eyes.

I quickly cleared my throat. "So how was your day?"

"Not bad." He flashed a grin that fucked with my pulse. "In the homestretch before retirement, so they don't expect a lot out of me right now."

"Wise on their part," I said with a laugh.

"You don't know the half of it."

"Uh, I knew you during your senior year. I know what a slacker you are on your way out."

Adam laughed. "Touché."

We talked about nothing for a good half hour, which raised my spirits considerably, and I found myself just a little bummed out when he sighed and said, "I should get going. Five o'clock comes early."

I wrinkled my nose. "Much too early."

He laughed. "Tell me about it."

"Well, think of me when you get up," I said. "I'll be sound asleep."

He raised an eyebrow. "Unless you get a wake-up call."

"Don't you fucking dare."

Adam smirked. "Or what?"

"Or I will have my revenge, and you know it."

He showed his palms. "Okay, okay. I'll behave."

"That'll be the day," I said with a snicker.

Laughing, he nodded. "You know me too well."

We looked at each other, neither speaking for a moment.

"Well, anyway," he said finally. "I should let you go. I'm glad you had a good time tonight."

"Thanks," I said softly. "I'll, um, talk to you later?"

He smiled, but it seemed forced. "Yeah. Ping me tomorrow night. I should be around."

"I'll do that."

Once again, we locked eyes, and the silence threatened to turn into a lengthy one, but then Adam said, "Well, good night."

"Good night," I said.

I clicked Disconnect, and the screen went dark. Then I shut the laptop and set it on the coffee table. Chewing my lip, I stared at the closed computer. We'd said our good-byes, but the conversation didn't feel complete. I couldn't sit still, couldn't relax.

Something needed to be said, and I wasn't going to sleep until it was.

I wanted to see him. It had only been, what, seventy-two hours? But I wanted to see him again.

"You also had a convenient excuse this time," I'd said when he'd suggested another visit, *"but what about next time? Are we really going to get together just for the hell of it?"*

Adam had looked into my eyes. *"Do we need a reason?"*

Well? Do we?

I grabbed my phone, and before I could talk myself out of it, I pulled up his number and hit Send.

"Hey," he said after one ring. "What's up?"

"I, um..." I cleared my throat. "Just forgot to mention while we were talking, I've got a three-day weekend coming up. Labor Day." I played with the edge of the cushion beside me. "I was thinking if you wanted to come up here, or I could go down there..."

My heart thundered. God, this was a bad idea. Friends, right? Just friends?

"I've got Labor Day off," he said quietly. "If you want to come down here, I'll pitch in for your ticket."

I swallowed. "I can pay for the ticket. Are you...are you sure?"

"Yeah. Yeah, of course. It'll be good to see you again. In person, I mean."

"Definitely. So I'll see you then."

I could tell from his voice that he was smiling as he said, "I'm looking forward to it."

After I'd hung up, I leaned back on the couch and stared up at the ceiling. There was no "maybe this is a bad idea" bouncing around in my head. Well, no "maybe" anyway. I knew damn well I was just tempting myself, and maybe even tempting him, and quite possibly setting myself up for a letdown.

But it wasn't like I'd committed to jumping his bones as soon as I got off the plane. We weren't doing strip clubs and body shots this time. I'd just feel him out. See how things went in person.

And hope for the best.

Chapter Eleven

My heart was going crazy well before the plane was on the ground. As soon as the flight attendant announced we'd be landing soon, I was in dire need of a gin and tonic. Or a Valium and tonic. Or a gin and Valium. That would've been fine.

I looked out the window and took a few deep breaths. Nothing was set in stone. Yeah, there'd been some weird—but hardly unfamiliar—tension between us ever since the night we'd decided this visit would happen, but that didn't mean anything. We weren't committed. Neither of us had said anything about the things that might happen when we saw each other—the things that had happened in the past when we'd seen each other—so as far as anything had been discussed, this was just another friendly visit. Adam would show me around San Diego, we'd spend a little time together, and then I'd go back to Seattle while our friendship stayed intact.

Yeah. I'll take that Diet Coke and Diazepam now, please.

The plane touched down, and I could have sworn the walk from the terminal to baggage claim was longer, but before I knew it, I was there. I'd only brought carry-on since it was just a weekend trip, so I went outside to wait for him.

Obviously unaware that I was nervous as fuck and wasn't quite ready to see him yet, Adam pulled up to the curb in front of me.

Here we go...

As I buckled my seat belt, I said, "Good to see you."

"You too. How was your flight?"

"Boring as ever." I sat back and shifted to get comfortable. "Just glad it wasn't longer, because it was a baby flight."

He grimaced. "Ouch. Those are brutal."

"Yes. Yes, they are."

The conversation died almost as quickly as it had started, and the radio played softly in the background as Adam navigated the twists and turns that led us out of the airport and onto one of the main roads. Once we were finally free of that clusterfuck, he picked up speed, and we headed into the city.

"So, um..." He rested a hand on top of the wheel and glanced at me. "Anything you'd like to see while you're in town?"

Just you.

I fidgeted a little. "Nothing in particular."

"I'd show you where I work, but it's pretty dull. And I can't take you into the building anyway."

"Building? I figured you'd be on a ship or something."

"Nah. I'm in my twilight tour." He glanced at me again, then added, "Means I'm getting close to retirement. I'd already made chief by the time I requested my last set of orders, so I didn't need to go to sea and bust my ass to make rank." He grinned. "So I'm kind of skating through to the end."

"Isn't that weird?" I asked. "Retiring at thirty-eight?"

He shrugged. "Well, it's not like I'll be put out to pasture or anything. Just done with the navy and ready to find another career."

"Seems like a big change this late in the game."

"This late in the game?" He chuckled. "It's not like I'm fifty."

"Well, not this year, no."

"Hey." He wagged a finger at me. "I've only got three months on you, so..."

"And when you turn forty, I will milk that three months for all it's worth."

"Color me shocked," he muttered. He pulled up to a stoplight and tapped his thumbs on the wheel. "So, I could, uh, take you by the hotel. You know, so you can check in while we figure out what to do with the rest of the afternoon."

"Sure. Yeah. Then maybe we can..." I racked my brain. "We can check out the rest of the city."

"All right. We can do that."

It took us twenty minutes to get to the hotel, and we bantered and made small talk the whole time. Nothing particularly deep, just playful ribbing in between the most benign commentary on the scenery and the city. Anything to keep me focused on something other than all the reasons I'd really wanted to come here, and how it just so happened that those were the same reasons I shouldn't have.

We're supposed to stay friends so things don't fall apart again.

Don't gamble with this.

What the hell are—oh, fuck it. I give up. I want him.

At least checking into the hotel gave me something to do for a minute so I could gather my thoughts. Of course, just my luck, there was no line and the clerk processed everything with lightning-fast efficiency. Bitch. Didn't she know I was taking a breather from some awkwardness out there in the car?

But I couldn't linger in here forever, so, key in hand, I went outside. My room was on the other side of the building, so Adam drove me around and parked right in front of the door.

As I reached back to get my bag out of the backseat, I paused. "Um, do you want..." I glanced at the door. Good idea? Bad idea? Fuck it. "Do you want to come in with me?"

Adam shrugged. The engine shut off, which answered my question, and I hoped to God he didn't hear my heart beating like crazy as we got out of the car and headed to the door.

Somehow, I got the key into the reader without dropping it or trying to do it sideways or something. I pushed open the door, and a blast of air-conditioning smacked me in the face as we stepped in from the Southern California heat.

"There's probably a guidebook or something in here somewhere," Adam said as the door clicked shut behind him. "Maybe we should thumb through that. See if there's anything that piques your interest."

I set my bag down on the dresser. "You know the city better than I do." Facing him, I added, "You tell me."

Our eyes met. Locked.

At the exact same time, we both cleared our throats and looked away.

Shit. Awkward silence. Must fix, must fix!

"Oh, and, um, thanks for picking me up, by the way," I said. "Cabs and rentals can be a pain in the ass."

"Any time." Adam shifted his weight from one foot to the other and back again but didn't look at me.

I couldn't remember ever seeing him so nervous. "What's wrong?"

"Nothing's wrong."

"But something's on your mind."

Adam kept his gaze down.

My heart beat faster. "Is there—"

"Why did you want to come down here?"

I gulped. "Because I...I wanted to see you?"

"So, just to visit, then." His eyes finally met mine. "Hang out."

I regarded him silently for a moment, trying to read his expression or figure out what might've been lurking in his guarded, flat tone. "Why else would I be here? We agreed to just be friends, right?"

"We did." He lowered his gaze. "Yeah, we did."

"So what are—"

"What would you do if I told you I wanted to kiss you?"

I almost choked on my own breath. "Since when have you ever asked before you kissed me?"

He cleared his throat. "Since we agreed to just stay friends, and I—"

I grabbed the front of his shirt and kissed him.

Adam shoved me up against the wall and took over the kiss, returning it even harder and hungrier than I'd given it, and thank God for that wall or I'd have melted at his feet.

"I don't want to fight this anymore," he whispered unsteadily. "I want you, Dale."

Any inhibitions I might've had crumbled. I opened to his kiss, moaning as his tongue slipped between my lips. Then, with shaking hands, I reached for his belt.

Adam didn't miss a beat, and neither of us held back. He pulled me toward the bed. We tumbled onto the hard mattress together. Shoes came off, and clothes, and we kissed and grabbed and clawed at each other. I straddled him, our hips grinding against each other as we breathlessly made out and pulled layer upon layer of fabric out of the way.

He tried to push me onto my back, but I shoved him down onto the mattress with a hand on his chest, and as I moved down toward his very erect dick, he swore under his breath. His fingers were already gripping handfuls of the sheets when I ran my tongue around the head of his cock, and as I took him deeper in my mouth, he moaned helplessly. He was thick enough to make my jaw ache, but I fucked him with my mouth and my hand. I'd been so confused earlier, but there were no questions when we were like this. When the lust was unbridled and we'd given our bodies free rein.

He tried to fuck my mouth, his hips jerking uselessly beneath my arm. "I need to fuck you," he moaned. "Oh Jesus, Dale..." He grabbed my hair tight enough to keep me from moving. "Please. You're gonna make me come, and I..."

I stopped and grinned as I looked up at him. "Let me get a condom."

He let me go. I lunged for my overnight bag, thanking several deities I'd had the foresight to bring both lube and condoms—you never know, right?—as I unzipped the pocket where I'd kept them.

Adam took them from me, and I squirmed with anticipation as he put the condom on.

"How should—"

"Hands and knees," he ordered.

Yes, sir...

I turned around. Closing my eyes, I bit my lip, ready to fall to pieces just waiting for him to fuck me. "Come on, come on..."

"I'm working on it." The lube bottle dropped onto the bed beside me. A moment later, Adam's slick fingers teased my anus, and my head spun as he gently worked them inside me.

"Just fuck me, Adam," I said. "Please. No games. I'm—"

His fingers slipped out. Then his cock pressed against me, and I moaned.

"Oh God," he breathed as he pushed deeper into me. "I've been wanting this since...fuck..."

I leaned back, impaling myself on him, forcing him into me until it was just this side of painful, and then a little harder because I couldn't wait. I dug the heels of my hands into the bed and thrust against him, desperate for him to fuck me as fast and deep as I could possibly take him. He met me thrust for thrust, slamming into my ass so hard my eyes watered. I lost track of time. I lost track of everything except how good he felt inside me, how painful his grip was on my hips and the way the whole world went white every time he bottomed out, and he drove me deeper into the most delicious state of pure ecstasy.

It was an overwhelming contradiction: the maddening tension of a building orgasm, and yet at the very same time, *relief*. How we'd gone so long without returning to this perfect, naked state. I didn't know, but this relief I felt now rivaled the bliss that would inevitably follow the orgasm that kept building, building, building.

Oh my God, Adam, I missed you so badly.

I don't want this to be over. I want to come.

I just want you.

Adam whimpered softly, then growled, and then he roared as he forced himself into me. His shudders were so violent, they reverberated all through my body, and I very nearly came too but remained on that precipice even as his climax ended.

"Turn over," he ordered as he pulled out, but he didn't give me a chance to comply. He shoved me onto my back, and before I could even catch my breath, he was over me and his mouth was around my cock. I was so close already, and the slick heat of his hand and lips and tongue were just too much, and in seconds, I thrust upward, into his mouth, and Adam groaned and I came so hard I damn near cried. My whole body shook— my whole world shook—and my orgasm was nearly as painful as his thrusts had been, and I loved every second.

Adam choked a little but still managed to swallow every last drop. Then he lifted off me, wiping his lip with the back of his hand. I sat up, grabbed him and kissed him. Deep and hard, moaning softly as I tasted myself on his tongue. He cradled the back of my neck, returning my kiss just as deeply.

That post-orgasmic lethargy started kicking in, and the kiss got lazier. Gentler. We both had just enough presence of mind to separate and clean ourselves up before collapsing together on the bed. He wrapped his arms around me, and I tucked my head under his chin and closed my eyes. He kept running his fingers through my hair, and the soft, rhythmic strokes threatened to put me to sleep. In fact, I did fall asleep for a little while, and I was pretty sure he did too.

As I stirred at one point, coming back out of a vague dream that I couldn't remember, Adam said, "Can I confess something?"

And with that, I was awake. My heart beat faster; was this the part where we told each other why we shouldn't have done this and shouldn't do it again? Before we'd even gotten out of bed?

I opened my eyes and looked up at him. "Will it obligate me to testify in a courtroom?"

Adam snorted. "No, it won't."

"Go ahead, then."

He laughed, but then turned serious. "I wanted... I wanted you to know..." *Here we go.* "You're the only man I've ever been with."

I blinked. "You're kidding."

"No." His cheeks darkened a little.

"You've...never been with another man. Ever."

Adam shook his head. "You were the first anyway, and then I was afraid to. DADT and all of that."

I searched his eyes. "Did you *want* to be with men?"

"Well, I..." He paused. "I thought about it. And I was certainly attracted to some guys along the way. Just never made it happen, I guess."

"You wouldn't know it," I said with a playful grin. "You seem to know what you're doing." *You can certainly turn my world inside out.*

He laughed. "I didn't say I was a virgin."

"Darling, I've had your cock in me a few too many times to make that mistake." *Shit. Draw attention to the number of times we've done this, and remind ourselves why we fought it for so long. Good one, Dale. Cue awkwardness...*

But Adam laughed. "You always were a classy one, weren't you?"

"Absolutely." I pushed myself up onto my elbow. "So, since you've never been with another man, I suppose it's safe to say you've never been fucked?"

He paled. "I, um, no."

"Should I take that to mean you wouldn't want to?"

"No," he said quickly. "Just means I've never done it." He eyed me nervously. "And I'm...not completely sure about it."

I swept my tongue across my lips. "Do you want to?"

He gulped. "Like, now?"

"Why not?" I put a hand over his. "If you don't, it's okay. But if you do..."

We looked at each other for a long, silent moment. I didn't know if he was working up the courage to say yes or to say no, or if he was just processing everything. I didn't know much of anything in that moment except how badly I wanted him again, right then, regardless of who was on top. Just thinking about it, I was already starting to get hard again. "Just tell me," I whispered. "If you want to or not."

Adam didn't say a word. He wrapped his arms around me, and we came together in a gentle, lazy kiss. He cupped my face in one hand, stroking my cheek with his thumb as he kissed me without all the earlier demands, but with all the hunger and desire. Our bodies sank together, and one brush of his hardening cock brought mine to full attention. I couldn't wait.

I pushed him onto his back and got on top.

He tensed, his whole body stiffening under mine.

"Relax," I said.

"I want... I... Just not sure..."

"If you don't like it," I murmured between kisses, "then I'll stop and you can fuck me."

"Mmm, I'm not going to turn *that* down," he whispered and relaxed into another long kiss.

"Turn over." I lifted myself off him. "On your hands and knees."

He eyed me warily but did as I asked.

I put some lube on my hand and then slipped it between his cheeks.

"What if I don't—ooh, holy *fuck*..." His whole body trembled as I teased his ass with my fingertip.

"Relax," I said and then ran the tip of my finger around his entrance again. I teased him until he did relax, and then I said, "Push back a little." When he did, I slipped a fingertip inside him. "You say stop, I'll stop." I slid my finger deeper, breaching that tight ring as he gasped. Slowly withdrawing my finger, I asked, "Should I stop?"

"*No.* Oh...God..."

"Just wait." I kept going with one finger for a little while, then pressed in a second. When he groaned, I asked, "You all right?"

"Mm-hmm."

I eased both my fingers into him a little at a time. He was tight but barely resisting. Hell, I'd been with experienced guys who offered more resistance than this, or at least flinched now and then, but Adam loved it. Right from the get-go. As I added a third finger to stretch him, he swore, gripping the sheets and rocking back against me, fucking himself on my hand.

I bit my lip. Fuck. Not only was he enthusiastic but good God, he really was *tight*. Just thinking about having my cock inside him made me crazy; I doubted I'd last long at all once I finally fucked him. It was a damned good thing I'd already come once or this would be over before it even got off the ground.

"Think you can handle—"

"Oh God, please." He shivered as he took all three fingers nearly all the way. "Fuck me."

Didn't have to tell me twice. "Stay just like that. I'll get a condom." I eased my fingers out and quickly put on a condom and some lube. As I stroked the lube onto my cock, I looked at him, checking his expression for signs of apprehension and finding none. Still, I asked, "You sure about this?"

Adam looked over his shoulder and gave me the hungriest, most mouthwatering grin. "*Fuck*, yes."

"Good," I said and positioned myself behind him.

At the touch of my cock to his ass, Adam whimpered. His whole body tensed, so I didn't move. He was stretched and prepped, but an inkling of panic or hesitation could quickly make this unpleasant for him, so I didn't rush. I waited until he relaxed, and then I pushed in a little. He took the head easily, and as I pulled back, he tried to come with me, tried to force me deeper. I could barely breathe as my cock sank into him. As he took more and more, I angled my hips so I was pretty sure I'd press against his prostate, and his whispered curses said I was right.

My vision blurred. My eyes rolled back. It wasn't just the fact that he was so amazingly tight. It was the fact I was fucking him. Fucking Adam. God knew how many fantasies had just concentrated themselves into this single overwhelming reality, and I couldn't think at all. The only thing I could do was move. Slowly. In and out, in and out, inching deeper every time.

I imagined myself fucking the hell out of him, driving in deep and hard and watching him take me over and over again, but the one thing I wanted more than that was to touch him. Touch as much of him as I could. I leaned down and rested my weight on one arm as I wrapped the other around him, holding him against me so his back heated my chest. Closing my eyes, I breathed him in, and I fucked him, and I completely lost myself in him. In his tight, virgin ass, in his primal, breathless growls, in the intoxicating scent of sweat and sex and him.

"Oh my God," he moaned. "That feels amazing."

I moved as slowly as I possibly could, sliding into him at glacial speed. "You want more than that?" I kissed the back of his neck. "Faster?"

He murmured something like an affirmative.

In his ear, I whispered, "I can't hear you, Adam. Do you want more?"

"*Yes.*"

I dropped another kiss on his neck and sat up again. Gripping his hips tight, I thrust into him hard and fast. There was no way I could fuck him as hard as he'd fucked me—I simply wasn't strong enough—but I gave him everything I had, and he cried out with ecstasy as he rocked back against me.

He shifted his weight onto his left arm, and I bit my lip as he reached under himself with his right. He tightened around me, both of us groaning as he stroked himself and I fucked him. God, he was too much. Usually I had to be careful with men who'd never done this before, but I swore if he could have spoken, he would have been demanding *more*.

His arm moved faster. I didn't think it was possible, but he tightened even more, and his whole body shook with an orgasm that was as silent as it was violent. I pulled his hips against mine, threw my head back and didn't make a goddamned sound as I fucking lost it. My whole body trembled against his, every wave of my climax sending another powerful shudder through me.

I cursed softly as I pulled out.

"Fucking Christ," he breathed. "If I'd known it was that good, I'd have tried it years ago."

I laughed as I took off the condom. "It's always a little intimidating the first time, but once you try it? It's amazing."

"Yeah, it is. Jesus."

After a quick shower together, we slipped into bed, facing each other. The second our eyes met, though, something sank in my gut. Oh. Right. We'd crossed some lines since we walked into this room, hadn't we?

I took a deep breath. "What are we doing?"

"I don't know," he said. "And to be honest, whatever it is, it scares the hell out of me."

"Why? If we keep gravitating toward each other, then maybe..."

Adam sighed. "I know. I get that up here." He tapped his temple. "But it took us this long to get back to each other, and my track record with relationships isn't good at all. That, and I'm still worried about ruining our friendship again."

"What do we do, then?" I asked.

"Take it a little at a time." He ran his fingers through my hair. "Just be patient with me. Maybe this will turn into more, maybe it won't, but I don't want to rush it."

"So we'll just be fuck buddies until we figure out if we can be more?" I sighed when I realized it sounded cattier than I'd intended. "Look, I'm fine with taking it slow. But friends with benefits is usually more benefits than friends, and we're...we're closer than that. I think?"

"Yeah. We are."

"So if I'm going to do this," I said. "Just be friends who sometimes have sex, you've got to meet me in the middle. I can't just be your occasional booty call when I care about you this much."

He swallowed. "Meet you in the middle, how?"

"I...just, give me a reason to believe there's a chance this could get off the ground." I made myself look him in the eyes. "That we're not just fucking until something better comes along."

"You're not a placeholder, Dale," he said, stroking my face.

"Then what am I?"

He held my gaze. Running his fingers through my hair, he said, "I don't know. You're my friend. You're..." He glanced down at our naked bodies, still sweaty and only half-covered by the sheet. "I can do that. I can meet you halfway. Let's just take this a little at a time and see where it goes, but for the moment"—he shook his head—"I can't do any more than this. I love the sex we have. You're a great friend who I've missed for a long time." He touched my face again. "I've been burned a few times. My marriages all ended badly. I've lost you a couple of times already. I'm not ready to lose you again."

"I'm not in this to hurt you, Adam." *You're the one who's left me before.*

"I know." He kissed me gently. "And I don't want to hurt you either. But let's not force this."

Does not forcing it mean not allowing it? But all I said was, "I can live with that."

"And in the meantime," he said with a grin, "we've got all weekend and a box of condoms. How badly do you want to see the city?"

"City?" I returned the grin and pulled him closer. "What city?"

Adam laughed as he rolled me onto my back. "That's what I thought."

Chapter Twelve

After San Diego, it didn't take long for us to find another excuse to see each other. In fact, we didn't bother with an excuse. We both had time, we both wanted sex, and I'd never been so grateful for cheap airfare in my life. At this rate, I was going to be racking up some crazy frequent flier miles.

So, less than three weeks later, after some racy Skyping and e-mails, Adam flew up to Seattle for a weekend.

So here he was again. In my world. On my turf. And there was no more pretense about being platonic friends. No pretense whatsoever, which was why my hips and legs weren't thrilled with me as Adam and I made our way into Safeco Field. Damn these ramps and stairs. Didn't they know I'd just gotten laid last night and again this morning? Jerks.

I didn't mention that to Adam, though. He also didn't need to know about the butterflies in my stomach. It had been years since I'd introduced a boyfriend to this gang, mostly because I hadn't had a boyfriend to speak of in ages. Well, okay, I'd had a few. But none who would have survived the bantering and ribbing from *this* group, which led me to wonder what the fuck I ever saw in those boyfriends to begin with. Big dicks only went so far.

Anyway, the guys had already met Adam. And for that matter, he wasn't a boyfriend. Just a friend with oh-my-God-hot benefits.

Only problem was, I was anything but objective when it came to Adam. My judgment was always cloudy when it came to him. With other guys, I was more aware than anyone if I hated his personality and was just in it for the dick, or if the guy was a sweetheart who was ridiculously incompatible with me in bed. I was pragmatic to the point of cold about it sometimes because, hey, life is short. I wasn't wasting it on guys who made me miserable, or lovers who couldn't—or wouldn't bother—to get me off.

With Adam, I... wasn't objective. I couldn't step back and look at our little arrangement and decide if I was setting myself up for a heartache, or if I was being cautious to the point I was going to push him away and regret it.

And if there was anyone in the world I could trust to tell me to get my head out of my ass—or Adam's dick out of my ass, one of the two—it was the four men sitting up there in the nosebleed section. If we spent a little time with them whenever he was in town, at least one of them would pull me aside sooner or later and tell me if they saw a problem. I was pretty sure Rhett still owed me for the number of times I tried to get *"stop being an idiot"* through his thick skull during the dark days a few years back, even if my advice *had* been *"just move on and let Ethan go before you drive yourself insane."*

"Hope you don't mind sitting in the cheap seats," I said.

"I don't mind at all." He glanced at me. "I'm just happy to be at a game. I haven't been to one in years."

I glanced back at him. "Since when?"

"Since I was stuck in Norfolk for my last tour," he said. "They don't even have a major league team."

"Really? Heathens."

"No kidding. I mean, they've got their minor league team, but it's just not the same."

"Well. No time like the present to make up for missed games."

"Agreed." He glanced upward. "I just have to ask, though, why in God's name would they have a retractable-roof stadium in this city of all places?"

I shrugged. "You'd be surprised. I've left a game or two with a hell of a sunburn."

"I don't think that'll be a problem today," he muttered, glancing up again at the very gray sky.

I was a little surprised the roof was open too. The anchormen must have predicted that the clouds would burn off later in the day. Or there would be enough "sunbreaks" —that term still amused me after living here all this time—to make it worthwhile to leave the roof open. At least the game wouldn't get rained out. If the skies opened up, they'd just shut the roof.

On the way up, we stopped at a concession stand to grab drinks.

As I paid for his beer and my soda, Adam said, "What? Coke? *You?*"

I laughed. "Ethan gets annoyed when I drink at games." I picked up my cup and shrugged. "I've been known to get a little, um, enthusiastic about the game when I'm drinking."

"I'd pay to see that," he said, chuckling.

"You can take that up with Ethan."

It was raining when we left the game. Pouring when we stopped for dinner at a swanky little café on Capitol Hill. And when we headed back to the car after dinner? Holy shit, it was coming down Noah's ark style.

"What the hell?" Adam shouted over the downpour. "I thought you said it didn't rain much here."

"I said it didn't rain as much as people claimed," I said. "I never said it didn't rain at all."

"Obviously there's some truth to the rumors."

"It rains everywhere eventually!"

He laughed, and we splashed through the water up to the stairs.

I pulled my keys out of my pocket on the way up, and muttered, "Finally."

"Wait." He caught my elbow with one hand.

I stopped and looked at him. "What?"

"As long as we're out here..."

Before I could make sense of what he was doing, Adam pulled me into an embrace and kissed me.

The world stood still. Rain still crashed down all around us, but everything else seemed to just...stop.

Cool water ran through my hair, down my face and under my collar, but Adam's body was warm through our wet clothes. His skin was hot to the touch, his kiss deep and passionate, and when I shivered, it wasn't from the rain.

My balance shifted. Adam pushed me up against the wall, and his kiss intensified as he pressed his body against mine.

I broke the kiss and looked in his eyes. Water slid down his temple, and a few drops clung to the ends of his hair before rolling down his cheek.

"I thought..." I struggled to find some breath. "I thought you didn't like the rain."

"No." He touched his warm forehead to mine. "I never said the rain was a bad thing."

"No, it's...it's definitely not always a bad thing." I cupped the back of his neck and drew him into another kiss. Though the water was cold and even the summer warmth couldn't temper that, Adam's body did. He was hot against me, his

143

fingers drawing warm lines across my cool, wet skin as he stroked my face and kissed me against the wall.

"I've been waiting all afternoon to do this," he said. "The rain was just a bonus."

"Why did you wait?" I asked, already out of breath. "Did you think—"

"Because I wouldn't have wanted to stop." He kissed me again, harder this time, and then murmured, "Let's go inside. Get out of these wet clothes."

I nodded. "Good idea."

My hands were shaking, but I managed to get the key in the door and let us into my condo.

We left our shoes by the door. Wet jackets landed with heavy smacks on the kitchen linoleum. Socks and shirts came off, but we only got as far as partially unbuckling his belt before we were too wrapped up in a kiss to peel off any more layers.

"You're shivering," he said. "Cold?"

"A little. You?"

He nodded. "Very. Shower?"

"Mm-hmm." Arms around him, mouth and half-naked body against his, I pulled him down the hall toward the master bathroom.

I let him go only so I could get the water running. As I reached in and turned on the shower, Adam did a double take in the other direction. "That is an impressive bathtub."

I glanced at the tub—a giant, sunken whirlpool that was just shy of being considered a hot tub—and then grinned at him. "Are you kidding?" I quirked an eyebrow at him. "I refuse to invest in a home that lacks a monstrous bath."

He wrapped his arms around me and kissed the side of my neck. "Well, as long as we're looking to warm up, maybe we should make use of that instead."

I turned off the shower.

While the bathtub filled up with steaming-hot water, we peeled off the rest of our clothes. We left them draped over the shower door to dry, and he eased himself into the tub. Once he was settled, I joined him, the warmth stinging my rain-cooled skin.

"You ever fool around in here?" he asked with a grin as he pulled me into his arms.

"Sex? In the bathtub? Why, no, I never thought of such a thing." I rolled my eyes. "Please, darling. This thing's been christened several times over."

"Maybe so." He tilted my chin up with his finger and leaned in closer. Just before he kissed me again, he growled, "But you've never had sex with *me* in it."

Oh. My God.

"So are you suggesting that since we've never fucked in here," I whispered, panting just from that kiss, "we ought to remedy that?"

"Do I think we should?" His warm laugh made me shiver as he dipped his head to kiss my neck. "I wasn't planning to leave this tub until I'd played out some of these images running through my mind right now."

"Oh yeah? Such as?"

"You'll see," he murmured and kissed me.

His hand glided down my chest beneath the water, then down my abs, and I arched toward him as he found my cock. He stroked me slowly, gently, coaxing my erection to its full hardness, all the while kissing me like he wanted nothing more in the world than to just feel and taste my lips and tongue with his.

I trailed my fingers down his chest and abs, shivering myself when his muscles contracted beneath my touch. We stroked each other under the water, and made out above it. The water and his body were hot against me, his kiss tender but still hungry.

When he broke that kiss, we were both out of breath, panting against each other's lips and still stroking each other beneath the surface.

"Oh God, I want you so bad, Dale," he whispered.

"I'm not going anywhere."

"Good." He bent and kissed my neck. I tilted my head back, letting him explore every inch of my throat. I stroked him a little harder, and he groaned against my neck, so I did it again.

I leaned away from him and felt around for the drain. When I pulled it open, Adam eyed me. "We're not getting out, are we?"

"No." I straddled him as the water level slowly went down around us. "Just letting the water out."

"Hmm, where's the fun in that?"

"Water doesn't bode well for"—I slid my cock against his—"lubrication."

"We don't have any lube, though," he said.

"Au contraire." I reached past him and plucked a small bottle off the shelf beside the tub. Holding it up, I grinned. "We have plenty."

He grinned. "And condoms?"

"Of course."

As the water drained around us, the air was a little cool on my wet skin, but the room was warm and Adam's body was even warmer. I pressed against him, slid my flesh across his and kissed him as we held each other closer. I moved over the top of him, straddling him so our dicks rubbed together.

"I want you to fuck me," I murmured. "Right here."

"Ooh, yes." He pulled me down against him, pressing his erection against me.

"But not yet. First..." I grabbed the lube off the side of the tub. "Give me your hand."

He held it out, palm up, and I poured some lube into it. Then I sat back a little, guided his hand between us and closed his lubricated hand around his hard cock. I thrust against him, sliding our dicks against each other inside his fist.

His other arm flew back. He grabbed the edge of the tub to brace himself. "*Jesus.*"

"Like that?"

"Ooh, yeah."

"Thought so." I thrust harder, fucking his hand and rubbing against his cock at the same time, and Adam groaned, his eyes rolling back.

Then he grabbed my hip to stop me. His hand left my cock and slid over my balls, then farther, and I spread my legs wider as his fingers slipped up against my asshole. He kissed my neck and teased me, and I sighed as two fingers slid into me.

I moaned, biting my lip and lowering myself onto him, searching for more of that penetration, that stretch. He added another finger. The slow, smooth strokes were *divine*, stretching me and pressing in just right to make my whole body tremble. I lowered my head and searched for, found and claimed a deep kiss from his mouth. I was more than ready for his cock, but I loved this. Making out with him, riding his hand while I stroked his huge erection. Our skin was slick and hot, our bodies sliding together without the slightest hint of unpleasant friction. I wanted him inside me, but I didn't want to separate. I wanted him to withdraw his fingers, guide his cock to me and just let me come down onto him, just like this.

I tilted my head back so he could get to any part of my neck he wanted. "Oh God, I want you to fuck me."

"Get a condom," he breathed. "I need to fuck you, Dale."

I didn't move. My heart quickened as a thought crossed my mind, and before I could think twice, I said, "I'm clean. Haven't touched anyone since I was tested last." My own words startled me, and, judging by the way his eyes widened, I wasn't the only one.

He swallowed. "The military tests me all the time."

I bent and kissed him, then murmured over my thundering heart, "I want you just like this. Without a condom."

"Are you...are you sure?"

"Yes," I whispered. "Yes. I trust you."

"I've never done this," he murmured. "Without... Uh, bareback."

"Neither have I." I kissed him again. "I want to, though. Are you sure you—"

"God, yes. Please, Dale." He looked up at me with wide eyes. "I want you. Just like this. Nothing between us."

"Yes," was all I could say.

I lifted up, and as I slowly came down, he guided me onto him.

Our watering eyes met, and his silently asked if I was sure.

Are you?

Why aren't you inside me yet?

The head of his cock pressed against my lubed, stretched ass, and as I lowered myself all the way onto him, he slipped into me, meeting almost zero resistance. He stretched me even more than his fingers had, but it wasn't the least bit uncomfortable. Quite the contrary. Holy fuck. As he hit that sweet spot, my vision blurred, and I shivered.

I rose slowly. My knees ached from sitting this way for so long, but who the hell cared? Adam was inside me, slick and uncovered, and I'd have knelt here until my knees bruised as long as I could feel us moving together like this.

As I came down again, his grasp tightened on my hips. He pulled me down onto him, so his cock was all the way inside me, and held me in place with warm, slippery hands.

"Oh God." He closed his eyes and rested his head against the edge of the tub. "Don't...don't move."

"I need to," I said, almost whimpering. "You feel so good, I—"

"If you move, I'll come," he whispered. "And then this'll be over."

I bit my lip and moaned. That he was so close to the edge was unimaginably arousing.

"Stay just like that." He licked his lips. Slowly, he looked me up and down. "God, you don't even know how hot you look, and feeling you like this..." He let his head fall back again as he groaned softly.

"I want to move," I slurred. "Adam..."

"You will. Just...just let me... Don't move yet." He swept his tongue across his lips again and then reached for the lube. He poured some more into his hands, and then his hands were on me, one stroking my cock, the other teasing my balls.

"Ooh... God..." I grabbed the edges of the tub beside his shoulders as a shudder rippled through me. His hands were so deliciously slick. He'd told me not to move, but goddammit, I couldn't stay still, and I rocked my hips just enough to keep him moving against my prostate and my cock sliding through his tight grip. This was a completely new and absolutely amazing sensation: being stroked, touched, stretched, filled, but unmoving. No thrusting. No deep, powerful strokes. Not even a slow, steady rhythm to drive me insane. He was simply *there*.

"Let me move," I breathed. "I want... I want..."

"Anything you want," he said. "I'm not ready for this to be over, but God, I want to make you come."

I whimpered and leaned down to kiss him. His hands slipped and slid on my skin. Sweat, lube, water; there wasn't an inch of dry skin on either of us. We kissed, we fucked, we moved together and held each other, and it was all smooth and fluid and so, so hot.

Adam shuddered. "Oh God," he breathed. "I'm gonna... I'm gonna come."

"I want you to," I said, my lips nearly touching his. "Come inside me."

"Will you let..." He whimpered and shuddered again. "Will you let me fuck you like this again? Bareback?"

"Let you?" I kissed him in between gasps for breath. Then I leaned past him and whispered in his ear, "Oh, Adam, I will *beg* you to fuck me like this again."

He responded with another soft whimper. I rode him harder, hard enough to drive both of us over the edge, and my own semen dotted his abs and chest as Adam came inside me.

We sank against each other. Adam wrapped his arms around me and rested his head against my chest. I held him as much as the tub behind him allowed, and for the longest time, we just stayed like that.

"You're shivering," he said after a while.

"Am I?" So I was. By now, the coolness of the room was settling onto my wet skin, and I was definitely starting to shiver. I lifted my head. "Why don't we get that shower, and then we'll get into bed?"

"I love that idea."

We showered enough to clean ourselves off and warm up. Then we moved into my bedroom and got under the covers.

Facing each other, we didn't speak. I touched his face, brushing the pad of my thumb across his cheekbone, and he held my gaze, but neither of us said a word. Something unspoken was trying to burn its way through my chest, but I couldn't think of anything to say that wouldn't be awkward or come out wrong or ruin this sublime moment.

So I kissed him.

Adam wrapped his arms around me, his hand between my head and the pillow as we melted together, two warm, naked bodies in no hurry to do anything except be just like this. We didn't feel each other up, or try to get each other turned on, we just...kissed.

Tomorrow, he'd be gone again. We'd be back to keeping the distance between us as small as possible through Skype and texts until we could be together again. I'd be back to wishing time would speed up instead of begging for it to slow down. And I'd be back to wondering how long this could go on before the other shoe dropped, before benefits went by the wayside and hopefully didn't take out our friendship as collateral damage.

But I'd deal with that tomorrow. Tonight, he was here.

And nothing else mattered.

Chapter Thirteen

Three visits in a row. Seattle. San Diego. Seattle again. He'd left this morning on another airport shuttle for his flight back to his own world, and now I found myself wandering aimlessly in a condo that was entirely too small for aimless wandering. Every time he left, I felt more gutted than the last time. Lost and empty, like I didn't know what to do with myself.

I scanned the contents of my refrigerator again, and still nothing looked appetizing. Earlier I'd taken a bottle of Merlot off the rack, but even that was still unopened. I was too wired for coffee, too *blah* for wine.

And it didn't make a damned bit of sense.

I mean, it wasn't like I didn't know this feeling. I knew this feeling. I knew it too well. That physically painful need to be with him. Ironically, the more my feelings for him transcended the physical and I wanted more than just his touch and his body, the more this ache became a real, tangible thing, something more than just a bummed-out feeling or a sense of loneliness.

None of which was compatible with our slightly-more-than-friends with slightly-more-than-benefits arrangement.

You're being pathetic, Dale, I told myself as I wandered idly into the kitchen for the hundredth time since I got home from work. *Since when do you ever get this hung up on a fuck buddy?*

Yeah, and since when did I have bareback sex? Ever? I'd always been weird about sex without condoms. Sure, I was confident I was clean, and I trusted him, especially since I knew the military tested their guys regularly, but condoms had always been nonnegotiable for me.

It hadn't been a premeditated thing that first time. One moment I'd been fooling around with Adam, and the next I'd wanted him inside me without a condom. It wasn't premeditated, but I couldn't even call it impulsive, because looking back, it still made perfect sense, both in the moment and in hindsight, and we hadn't used a condom since.

I'd slept with plenty of men, and I'd had relationships with quite a few too, but I'd never experienced intimacy to that degree. And it wasn't the bareback sex that made it that intimate. Foregoing a condom had simply been a natural progression. Merely a hat tip to the closeness, the trust, the feelings that already existed.

Except Adam wanted to be friends, and nothing more.

"Are we just friends?" I'd asked sometime late last night. "We're flying back and forth, fucking the nights away. Is what we're doing really just friends with benefits?"

He'd shrugged. "Do we need to call it something else?"

I'd let it go. No point in arguing. I wasn't going to push him into a premature commitment or anything like that. I just wanted to know...something. Sure, we could fuck bareback and dive into a level of intimacy I hadn't known existed, but that hadn't really changed the definition of our relationship.

"We've got something really good going on right now," he'd said this morning. "If it isn't broken, why fix it?"

But what if it is broken? What if my feelings for you aren't even in the same ballpark as yours for me?

Though, did it even matter? Even if he wanted more, did I dare let my guard down after the last couple of times? Making relationships last obviously wasn't a strong point of his, and my empty condo was evidence enough that I'd never been very good at that myself.

I glanced at my laptop, which was closed and silent on my coffee table. Adam would be home from work soon, and we usually talked for a while on the webcam when we were both home, but I wasn't sure I could face him tonight.

Not that I had much choice, though. As luck would have it, tonight was Sabrina's engagement party. Maybe socializing would help me get my head out of my ass.

Stay home and hash things out with Adam?

Go party with Ethan and Rhett?

Well, *that* was a tough choice.

When I arrived, Rhett and Ethan's house was packed. I recognized a few people from parties I'd attended here before— some family, some friends, a few of both of their coworkers—but there were plenty of new faces too. Young, most of them, so I suspected they were Sabrina's friends and classmates. Considering she was getting ready to graduate from college, and most of her friends looked like they were about thirteen, I must have been getting old. I could only imagine how Ethan felt in this crowd.

Speaking of whom, I found Ethan in the kitchen, where he was pouring wine for himself and Kathy, Rhett's ex-wife.

"Kathy!" I held out my arms. "I haven't seen you in ages!"

"Oh, Dale!" She hugged me and then stepped back and looked me up and down. "Looking fabulous, as always."

I rolled my eyes. "Would you expect any less from a gay man?"

"Well..." Her gaze slid toward Ethan.

His jaw dropped. "What? I look fine."

She patted his arm. "Of course you do, honey."

"What's that supposed to mean?"

"Nothing, Ethan. Nothing at all."

He grumbled something I didn't understand.

Kathy ignored him. She looked toward the living room, where Sabrina and Rhett were talking to a guy who I assumed was Tyson's dad. The resemblance was pretty damned strong, and the man had enough gray hair to have raised someone who'd marry a child of Rhett's.

Kathy shook her head and sighed. "I cannot believe my little girl's getting married."

"No kidding," Ethan said. "I could've sworn she was just going to prom."

"Prom, hell," Kathy said. "I think I'm still on freeze-frame from when she started high school."

Chuckling, Ethan raised his glass. "You said it."

She clinked her glass against his. "I just hope she doesn't make me a grandma quite yet. I don't think I could handle that."

Ethan's eyes widened.

"Don't worry." Kathy winked. "I made her promise to wait until I'm at least forty-five."

"At least forty-five?" Ethan stared at her. "Are you suggesting that's the cutoff for when someone should become a grandparent?"

I snorted. "Ethan, Ethan, Ethan." I patted his shoulder. "You're an old man. Just accept it."

"Fuck you," he muttered into his glass.

Kathy and I both laughed.

After a little more chitchat, I politely excused myself from the conversation to mingle with some of the other guests.

It didn't take long to run into Kieran, who was looking stylish and gorgeous as always. Son of a bitch could make jeans and a T-shirt look amazing, but he'd gone with a gray button-up shirt and black slacks tonight. Fabulous, which seemed to be the kid's natural state.

"Hellooo, Kieran," I said. "You didn't have to work tonight?"

He shook his head. "Though the ironic thing is, one of the few nights I have off work that I'm not spending on wedding crap, I'm at a party for someone else's wedding." He rolled his eyes and sighed.

I laughed. "Oh, come on, it can't be that bad, can it? It's still months away, anyway."

"Trust me, it's a headache. Thank God we're not having a huge wedding because this one is a big enough pain in the ass."

"How is all that going, anyway?" I asked. "I mean, that's got to be hard on Alex, getting married without his family around."

Kieran grimaced. "Yeah, it's been rough. And I've told him we can just go down to the courthouse if that's easier, but he really wants to have our friends and, well, my family there." He paused. "He has been talking to his brother recently, though."

"Really? How is that going?"

"It's...a process. But I think they're working things out. There's been some talk about him flying out here to see Alex and meet me soon."

"Oh, well, good. That's a step in the right direction. Think the rest of the family will ever come around?"

"Maybe, maybe not. At this point, Alex is happy just to have some communication with his brother again. They were really close before all this went down, and I think it's been good for him."

"That's good to hear," I said.

Kieran smiled. "Yeah. I think there's hope for them yet. Maybe not the rest of the family, but...it's a start."

"Well, good. One step at a time."

We continued chatting and mingling, and after a while, I slipped into the kitchen to refill my wineglass. As soon as I was alone, I paused to stretch some stiffness out of my neck and shoulders. Why was I so exhausted already?

Oh. Right. Alcohol plus no sleep. That, and I was starting to think maybe I wasn't in the mood for a party after all. The festive atmosphere was usually my thing, the kind of world where I flourished, but tonight it was weighing more heavily on me than it should have been.

With my wineglass full, I slipped out the sliding glass door onto the balcony—which was mercifully deserted—to get some air. Leaning on the metal railing, I gazed out at the Space Needle, since it was a convenient focal point in the night sky.

Even a party at Rhett and Ethan's couldn't get my mind off things. That was unusual. And this wasn't like me at all. Yeah, I liked to get myself infatuated with men I couldn't have, but not to this extent. Not to the point I hadn't had a decent night of sleep in weeks, especially since I barely slept after every time Adam left.

But there usually wasn't so much at stake. I never had friendships on the line when I actually got involved with men, because I didn't date my friends unless I was absolutely certain we could fuck without things getting weird.

When this started, I'd asked him to meet me halfway. This could be friends with benefits, but I needed a little more than that. I could have sex with him, but I'd needed to know I wasn't *just* a booty call for him. That I wasn't just a convenient piece of ass until he found something he wanted to keep around for a while.

He hadn't given me any reason to believe he was using me. In fact, there were moments when I was sure he felt *something*. Like when we'd had sex in my tub, when we'd gone bareback without any hesitation and it had felt so damned perfect, he'd been right there with me on the same wavelength. Every time we touched, it was like we were so much more than what we'd agreed to be.

But we didn't acknowledge it. We didn't talk about it much. We didn't give it a name. What happened if we did? Would it all just go away?

Or, more to the point, would *he* just go away?

The sliding glass door opened behind me. I subtly cleared my throat just to make sure my voice was steady if anyone expected me to speak, and then I glanced over my shoulder.

"Oh, hey," I said as Ethan closed the door behind him.

"Hey, yourself." He faced me. "You doing okay?"

"Yeah." I pasted on a smile. "Of course. Why?"

"You tell me."

I swallowed.

"You're not yourself tonight." Ethan rested his elbow on the railing and sipped his wine. "Something wrong?" He paused. "Is this about Adam?"

I lowered my gaze. "Yeah."

"I figured. Things aren't going well?"

"They're going great," I said. "That's...that's kind of the problem."

"What do you mean?"

I rubbed my forehead with my thumb and forefinger. "It's weird, though. In the bedroom, I—" I paused, glancing at him as heat rushed into my cheeks. "That's not TMI, is it?"

Ethan chuckled. "With all the comments we've made about fooling around with Kieran?" Shrugging, he brought his wineglass to his lips. "Don't worry about it."

I laughed softly. "Okay, so in the bedroom, I trust him. Completely. I've always felt safe with him."

"You mean physically safe."

"Right."

"What about emotionally?"

Sighing, I folded my forearms on the railing and leaned over them. "When I'm with him, yes. I do. It feels perfect. And safe, yes." I lowered my gaze into the dark shadowy void below us that was Ethan and Rhett's backyard. "It's when I'm not with him that I don't know what to feel."

"Have you guys talked about this?"

I threw him a look.

Ethan laughed cautiously. "I'll take that as a no."

"You'd be right."

"Well, why don't you talk to him?"

I've tried. Maybe not hard enough, but I've tried.

I gnawed my lower lip. "Would you think less of me if I said I was scared to death?"

"Not at all," Ethan said with almost uncharacteristic gentleness. "I understand completely. I also know how much it can cost someone to give in to that fear."

I unfolded my arms and lifted myself up a little, resting my weight over my hands. "I'm sure you're familiar with the idea of the one that got away."

"Familiar?" Ethan glanced in through the sliding glass door, then gave me a pointed look. "You saw yourself how close I came to letting him get away."

"I remember," I said.

"So you feel like Adam is the one that got away?" he asked. "Even though you're together?"

"We're not really together. That's the thing." I blew out a breath. "Maybe there's a reason he got away in the first place."

"It's possible," he said. "Or he may just need some time to realize you're the one who got away from him."

I ran my fingers back and forth along the wrought iron railing, but didn't speak.

"You guys have been apart for a long time," Ethan went on. "It took you this long to come back together, so give yourselves some time to figure out if it's right or not. You don't want to rush into a relationship, but don't rush out of it, either."

I sighed. "I keep telling myself that, but I'm impatient, I guess. And...honestly, even though we were kids the first time things didn't work out, and he was trying to salvage his marriage the second time, I...I guess I'm just worried in the end I'll have nothing but a shitload of regrets and frequent-flier miles."

"Then maybe that's what you need to tell him," Ethan said. "You're not demanding a ring or anything. Just, you know, get on the same page." He put a hand on my shoulder. "Just talk to him."

I nodded. "I will."

"Good." His hand didn't move. "You'll be all right?"

I nodded. "Yeah. Thanks."

He squeezed my shoulder gently before he let go and started for the door.

"Hey, Ethan."

He turned around, eyebrows up.

"When did you know?" I nodded past him. "That Rhett was the one?"

Ethan looked over his shoulder at Rhett. Then he turned back toward me. "When by all rights it should have been too late."

"You mean, after you guys broke up?"

He nodded. Turning to watch his husband again, he said, "I knew I wanted to be with him all those years before we started falling apart, but it wasn't until we'd split up and he was as good as gone that I *knew*." He looked at me again, his haunted expression giving me chills. "And believe me when I tell you I'm thankful every single day that we gave each other a second chance."

I nodded. "I believe you."

"Talk to him, Dale," Ethan said a little unsteadily. "If Rhett and I had done more of that, I think we would have avoided a lot of things."

I nodded again but didn't speak.

"And hey," he said. "Whatever happens, you know we're always here."

I smiled. "I know. Thanks."

He returned the smile. "Don't stay out here too long. There's a party going on. You're supposed to be having a good time."

"Yeah. Yeah, I know. I'll, um, just give me a few minutes."

He eyed me skeptically but then nodded. "All right."

Ethan went back inside. As I watched, he crossed the living room to where Rhett was talking to their future son-in-law. He put an arm around Rhett's waist, and, without even missing a beat in the conversation, Rhett slid a hand into Ethan's back pocket.

They made it look so easy. So natural. And I knew as well as many of the people in that room just how horrible things had been between Ethan and Rhett before they broke up. During the months leading up to that split, I never would have believed anyone if they'd told me those two would ever be back on speaking terms, never mind happily married and stronger than ever.

I turned around and looked out at the city again.

I wanted what they had. What Ethan and Rhett had, and what Alex and Kieran had. I wanted that so bad it physically hurt to think about it. But was I wasting my time with a man who didn't want any of that? Or, more to the point, a man who didn't want any of that *with me?*

I couldn't make myself stop being attracted to Adam, and while I'd never had a problem with casual sex, I couldn't separate physical from emotional when it came to him. He was the one man in the world I couldn't casually fuck without getting tangled up emotionally, and the last two attempts to do so had ended in disaster. And this time, it wasn't an impulsive one-night stand. We'd invested more this time.

I closed my eyes and took a deep breath.

We'd talk. God knew what conclusions we would come to, but the next time we were both online, we'd discuss this.

I wasn't interested in giving him ultimatums. I just needed to know something. Hell, maybe an ultimatum *was* in order. This whole thing was making me crazy, and something had to give before I crumbled under the weight of it all.

But I'd give him a chance. I'd keep an open mind and a cautiously open heart. If it didn't work, if he didn't meet me halfway like I'd asked him to do, then I'd show him to the door and move on with my life. Yeah, it might hurt, but then I would know. I would have closure.

Or maybe I'd finally have the chance to fall in love with him. Find out what it was really like to be what we could have been before if things had happened differently.

And if I do fall for you, Adam, especially if I've fallen for you already like I think I have, please, please don't break my heart again.

Chapter Fourteen

I'd promised myself—and Ethan—that I'd talk to Adam. And I would. Eventually.

One conversation on the webcam went by. Then another. We talked every night that week except for one when he had to work late. The following week, same thing.

Tonight. I'll do it tonight.

I steeled myself. Had a glass of liquid courage. Gave myself a lecture and told myself we would work this out and figure out what the hell we were doing, and we would do that tonight.

AdamO wants to connect.

I took a deep breath, reminded myself that I needed to do this, and clicked *accept*.

Adam's face appeared on the screen. He smiled.

My heart skipped, just like it always did when I saw his face. And—surprise, surprise—all my resolve disappeared.

We chatted about our days at work. He told me about some sailors who'd gotten into trouble over something stupid, and the ridiculous amount of paperwork he'd had to do. I told him about how the senior architect threw a shit fit over some dimensions but then realized he was wrong and issued an apology in the form of, *"Well, make sure you don't screw up the dimensions."*

After a while, Adam had to call it a night since he had to get up early the next morning, the poor bastard. Just as we were about to disconnect, though, he said, "Oh, wait. One more thing before you go."

"Hmm?"

"I meant to ask before, and I know it's short notice, but I'm... My retirement is coming up in a couple of weeks. And I'd really like you to be there."

A voice in the back of my mind screamed at me not to commit to going, not until we'd had a chance to work some things out, but I ignored it and my good sense.

"Sure, I'd love to."

"Great." He smiled, and I swore he seemed relieved that I'd agreed to it. Did he really think I wouldn't? Then he said, "By the way, fair warning—my mother will be there."

I cringed. "I'm guessing she's still not keen on 'flaming little fairy boys' like me?"

Adam laughed. "Afraid not."

"Don't worry. I'll behave."

"That's not what I meant. I just figured I'd give you a heads-up in case you'd be uncomfortable."

"I don't think I could ever be completely comfortable around her, but... You do want me to come to this thing, right?"

"It would mean a lot if you did."

"Then I'll be there."

Adam smiled. "Great. I'm looking forward to it."

"I'll bet you are," I said, chuckling. "You're *retiring*."

"Yeah, and—" He cut himself off. "Yeah. Getting the hell out of this job."

"Well, just e-mail me the details, and I'll make my travel arrangements at work tomorrow."

"All right, sounds good. I'm going to call it a night. For some reason, they still expect me to come in at o'dark thirty in the morning." He sighed and rolled his eyes.

I laughed. "Bastards."

"No kidding. Anyway, have a good night."

"You too."

We disconnected, and I rested my elbows on my knees, hands clasped beneath my chin. Well, I'd failed. Again. And now we were going to see each other again. There was a date. A plan. A countdown between now and then. Question was, what about all this shit I had on my mind? Hash it out before that? Discuss it in person? Wait until after his retirement?

Dale Ramsey. Grow some goddamned balls before the stress gives you an ulcer.

I put my face in my hands and groaned. Really? I'd just committed to seeing him again—at his retirement, no less—and hadn't made a damned bit of progress toward figuring out what the hell we were doing. So that was three more weeks of avoiding this conversation. Or at least avoiding doing more than just scratching the surface like we'd done tonight.

I sat up. No. This was bullshit. I was not going to mope for the next few weeks and put myself and my happiness on hold for him. There was no way I was letting myself get hung up on someone who I couldn't have. Not again. I'd been down that road before, with him and with other men, and I *always* wound up falling on my face. Not this time. And not with him again.

I was also not sitting at home and feeling sorry for myself.

I went back to my bedroom to change clothes. I found a pair of black pants that fit just right, and a blue shirt that had gotten me laid *numerous* times. A good half hour in front of the mirror later, and after a spritz of that cologne that was just to die for, I grabbed my cell phone and keys.

Normally, I'd walk. It was only a few blocks, after all. But I didn't want to be sweating when I walked through the door, so I summoned a cab.

I slid into the backseat. "Wilde's on Broadway, please."

Not five minutes later, he dropped me off under the club's familiar neon sign. I paid him, and then went inside, paid my cover and scanned the full room.

When it came to fitting large quantities of the absolute hottest members of Seattle's gay community, Wilde's never failed to deliver. The bar, the booths and *oh,* that dance floor were crowded with some of the sexiest available men in this town. And nobody came to Wilde's to find Mr. Right. No, this was the place they came for Mr. Right Now over the Hood of a Car in the Parking Lot after a Couple of Cosmopolitans. Not that I knew from experience or anything.

The irony was that at least three of the bartenders were wearing wedding rings, and I knew one in particular who would be wearing one in a few months. I wasn't interested in serious relationships tonight, though. Give me a drink, give me a look, and meet me in the parking lot with a condom and your O-face.

I went up to the bar. Kieran was working tonight, so I found a barstool near where he was pouring drinks for a gorgeous blond guy. He glanced at me and did a double take. Once he was finished with his customer, he came to me.

"Dale?" he said. "I didn't expect to see you here tonight."

I shrugged, wondering when my muscles had gotten so damned tight. "Just needed an evening out."

"Right, but there's an evening out, and there's"—he gestured at our surroundings—"an evening out."

"Yes. Yes, there is."

"I thought you and your guy in California had a thing."

"Just a Kamikaze, please." Kieran was, after all, known for his Kamikazes.

His eyebrows rose, but he didn't protest. He mixed the drink and slid it across the bar but refused my money.

"Okay," he said. "Out with it. What's wrong?"

I stared into my glass.

"Dale. Come on. You haven't been yourself lately, and you haven't been *here* in ages. What's up?"

Lifting my gaze, I smirked. "So is this the part where I pour my heart out to the bartender?"

Kieran laughed. "You wouldn't be the first, but you're my friend, so...you're not leaving until you do."

I laughed too, but with less enthusiasm. Then, sighing into my drink, I said, "Yeah, okay, I've been stressed."

"Adam?"

I nodded.

"What's going on? Did you guys break up?"

"We didn't...break up. We're not really even together. I just think I'm a little more into him than he is me, let's put it that way." I raked my fingers through my hair. "Why am I still so fucking hung up on him?"

Kieran reached across the bar and squeezed my arm. "Maybe the question is, why are you fighting it so hard?"

"Fighting it?" I looked at him, eyebrows up. "I've been carrying a torch for him for twenty years."

"Well, maybe there's a reason for that. I'm not a big believer in fate or any of that, but if neither of you can let it go after this long..."

"I don't know if I'd say *neither* of us can let it go," I muttered. "And besides, do you really think I should stick it out just because it's been going on this long?"

"Absolutely not. My parents split after like thirty years together, and it should have happened years before that." Kieran took his hand off my arm. "But there was definitely a spark between you two in Vegas, and that day we all went to the game, and every time I've seen you since. So I think it's at least worth thinking about why you two keep gravitating back to each other. Maybe the reason you come up with will be the reason you let yourself be with him. Or, maybe, the reason you put it to rest and move on."

I said nothing.

"What is it about him that keeps you going back?" Kieran asked. "I'm assuming it's more than his bedroom skills."

I shivered. "Well, he's certainly good in that department..."

Kieran chuckled. "That's a plus. But what else? What do you see in this guy?"

I looked up at the top-shelf bottles behind him, watching the dance floor lights play on the colorful labels and liquors. "We've just always had this...connection. We were close all through school, and..." I sighed. "Honestly, I think I was in love with him for a long time, but since I thought he was straight, I ignored it."

"So you guys were friends, and then..." He cocked his head, lifting an eyebrow.

I filled him in on my sordid history with Adam, from the friendship to the crush, to the night we fucked on the beach and the night we spent together after our ten-year reunion. And, of course, everything from our twenty-year reunion until tonight. Just rehashing it all was exhausting and reminded me why I was here to begin with. Took two Kamikazes to get through it all too. Which I supposed should have told me something. If just talking about the relationship, such as it was, was that draining, maybe it wasn't such a healthy thing to keep doing.

Once I'd reached the end—and was halfway through my third Kamikaze—I said, "Anyway, I'm heading down to San Diego for his retirement soon. I guess he and I can talk about all of this when I get there. Or after his retirement."

Kieran nodded. "Or maybe before that."

"I don't know about—"

"Dale, you're only ripping yourself apart by keeping this quiet. If you tell him how you feel, and he doesn't feel the same way, that doesn't mean you're going to lose him forever. If it does, maybe you didn't need him in your life to begin with. But you can't let this keep eating you alive."

"Fair point." I looked into my glass, then pushed it away and looked out at the dance floor. As I scanned the crowd of gyrating, jaw-dropping hot men, my heart sank lower with every gorgeous ass and perfectly flat stomach I saw. Sighing, I faced Kieran again. "You know, I don't think I'm in the mood to be here after all. I'm going to head out."

"Okay." Kieran eyed me, chewing his lip. "You know, Alex is home tonight. Do you want me to have him give you a lift?"

"Sure, why not?"

"Hang tight for a minute." He sent Alex a text. Then he flagged down a sandy-blond guy behind the bar. "Hey, Liam. Stepping out for a minute."

A guy gave him a sharp nod, and Kieran and I slipped out the back of the club. We followed the sidewalk around to the side of the building.

"Alex will meet us out here," he said.

"You don't have to wait with me. If you need—"

"You think I'm going to turn down a chance for a break?"

I chuckled. "Fair enough."

I sat on the curb. Kieran sat beside me, apparently not worried about getting anything on his immaculate black tux pants.

"Thanks for listening, by the way," I said.

"Any time. That's what bartenders are for, right?"

We both laughed quietly.

"You sure you'll be all right?" Kieran asked. "I've never seen you this upset over a guy."

Because you didn't know me ten and twenty years ago.

"I'll be fine," I said. "I hope."

"What do you think you'll do if the...if the conversation doesn't go well?"

I tilted my head back and looked up at the night sky. "I don't know. I mean, I know if he walks away from me over this, I should let him go. But I'm scared to death of losing him again. I love him. I..." *God, I do, don't I? I do love him.* I exhaled hard. "On one hand, I think it'll hurt like hell to be around him as a friend if he knows I feel that way and he doesn't feel the same. On the other..." I shook my head. "Fuck, I don't even know."

Kieran squeezed my arm. "Whatever happens, you know you can always call if you need to."

I put my hand over his and patted it gently. "Thanks. I appreciate it."

A moment later, a car pulled into the parking lot, and Kieran gestured toward it. "There's Alex."

We both stood and dusted ourselves off.

The car stopped in front of us, and Alex left the engine idling as he got out. "Hey. Everything all right?"

"Yeah," I said. "Just had a few to drink, and now I'm thinking this isn't where I need to be tonight."

He gave me a puzzled glance and then shifted it toward Kieran but didn't say anything. I suspected Kieran would fill him in on the basic info later that evening. They exchanged a quick kiss before Alex and I got in the car.

Alex looked at me across the console. "So, um, as long as we're out, do you want to grab a cup of coffee or something?"

"Sure, why not?"

He took me to a hole-in-the-wall diner-slash-coffee shop a few blocks from Wilde's. It was a place I'd been to before, one of those dives that probably hadn't changed its menu since it opened. At least it was quiet and the coffee was good.

Over a couple of slices of apple pie and some coffee, I gave Alex the rundown of everything I'd told Kieran.

"Wow," he said. "Sounds like a hell of a headache."

"Nature of the beast for relationships."

"I don't know about that." He shrugged. "But then, I'm not much of an expert on relationships." He laughed self-consciously. "Only had one."

"You don't know how lucky you are." I absently stirred my coffee. "You got it right the first time."

"Do you think *you* might've gotten it right the first time?"

I furrowed my brow. "What do you mean?"

"Well, I mean, I don't know if Adam was your *first* or not, but maybe you guys had it right twenty years ago. Maybe you were meant to be, and that's why you keep gravitating toward each other."

Laughing bitterly, I shook my head. "I don't know. Unless the third time's the charm. The first two times blew up in my face, and so far this time isn't looking promising."

"Maybe that's only because you guys haven't gotten on the same page."

"Maybe."

"You know, Kieran and I had to go down that road." He cradled his cup of coffee in his hands, like he was trying to warm them up. "We both had feelings that went beyond being friends with benefits, and we had to, you know, go there."

"Except I don't know if he feels the same way."

"And I didn't know if Kieran did. He didn't know if I did." Alex set his coffee cup down. "In fact, Kieran pretty much disappeared on me for a while before he finally got his head together, and when he came to talk to me, we both thought it was over."

I took a sip of coffee and rolled it around on my tongue for a moment before I swallowed it. "And if that conversation had gone badly and you guys had split up, but then came back together, how many times do you think you would have let it fall apart before you called it a loss and walked away?"

Alex shook his head. "I have no idea. Looking at it at the time, I'd have told you once was enough. Now that I've seen what Kieran and I can do once we hit our stride, I'd go through that shit as many times as it took to bring this back."

That knocked the breath out of me. If there was anything I wanted from a man, it was knowing our relationship was worth going to hell and back to save. I wanted someone for whom I'd be willing to do that, and I wanted someone who was willing to do that for me.

And no matter how much I wished it weren't the case, I couldn't make myself believe I was that man for Adam.

Mirroring Alex, I wrapped both hands around my coffee cup. "You know what the hardest part about this is? When we go through all the motions, and I can actually make myself believe we're doing romantic shit. That we *mean* it."

"Do you mean it?"

I nodded. "I do, yes."

"Does he?"

"That's what I don't know. And I don't want it unless he means it."

"I don't blame you."

"I'm not even sure what we're doing, to be honest with you, or why I'm so hung up on him. We have amazing sex. We enjoy each other's company. But I... When it comes to him, I need more than that. Maybe that's a double standard. I don't know.

If I want sex, I can go to out and find sex. If I want someone to hang out with, I've got you guys." Blowing out a breath, I leaned back in my chair. "I don't know, maybe we need to take a little breather from each other just to let the dust settle."

"That's probably not a bad idea."

"Only thing is, we're so far apart," I said. "And the long distance thing, I... I just don't want us to become Facebook friends and nothing more. You know, the people who see each other on Facebook but never actually interact. If what we've been doing the last few months is out of the question, then I can live with that, but I want more than...*that*."

"Then that sounds like something you should tell him."

I nodded. "I should." Sighing, I shook my head. "God, I miss the way we were before we graduated. When we were friends. To be honest, I'd rather have him as a friend than not at all. In fact, I want—" I paused, searching for some air, and finally whispered, "I want that back more than I want this." My own words hit me hard in the gut, the truth grabbing hold and refusing to let go. My feelings for him ran so much deeper than friendship, and the thought of losing him as a lover didn't hurt nearly as much as the thought of losing him completely.

"Do you think you guys can go back to that?" Alex asked.

"I hope so." I sighed. "Feels like I'm the one who'll have to figure that out, not him."

Alex cocked his head. "What do you mean?"

"I mean, I think he'd be okay with just being friends." Another kick in the gut. "The attraction is there, but beyond that, I think I've always wanted more out of this than he did, and he's had to make decisions in his life that didn't always mean staying with me. I'm not holding that against him. His career and what we could have been, they were never compatible. We both knew that."

"But you can't be someone's second choice, Dale."

I flinched. "Should he have put his whole life on hold because of a one-night stand between a couple of high school graduates?"

"Not necessarily. But you guys were friends, right?"

"Close ones, yeah."

"Okay, and it still sounds like he just walked away. You guys slept together, and then he was gone. And the second time?" He raised his eyebrows.

I exhaled hard and rubbed the back of my neck. "We slept together, and then he was gone, but he was trying to save his marriage."

Alex didn't respond. His eyes lost focus, and he chewed his thumbnail.

I cocked my head. "What?"

He lowered his hand and looked me in the eye. "I may be out of line with this, and feel free to ignore everything I say, but can I be completely candid?"

"Please do."

He took a deep breath. "I think you need to do more than just talk to him and find out what he's feeling and what he wants. I think *you* need to tell *him* what you want and what you need." He inclined his head slightly, holding my gaze. "Don't be a doormat, Dale."

I opened my mouth to insist I wasn't, but hesitated. *"Am I being a doormat?"*

"Not necessarily," he said. "But you're talking a lot about what he wants and what he needs, not to mention what choices he's made. What about you? You're in this too. I just want to make sure that if your wants and needs don't line up with his, you're willing to walk away rather than compromise yourself."

My heart sank deeper and deeper in my chest.

Alex kept his voice soft and gentle as always. "He wanted that career, and he wanted to make his marriage work. I don't think any of us can blame him for that." He paused for a moment, looking in my eyes, and when he spoke again, his voice was quiet. "But none of that changes the fact that you're the guy he left in the dust both times. You were the backup, the fallback." He paused. "You were his second choice."

I winced.

Alex went on. "I don't know him like you do. I'm only telling you how it looks from where I'm standing. And from where I'm standing, you were the guy he went to when he was about to leave for the navy. Then you were the guy he went to when he thought his marriage was over. And now you're the guy he's with when he's about to retire. Now that the career he always wanted is over." Alex folded his hands on the table. "It sounds to me like this guy always comes back when his life is in flux."

My stomach twisted itself into an uncomfortable knot. "So you think he just came to the reunion to find me because he was single now and he didn't have to worry about the navy anymore?"

"Am I wrong?" Alex moistened his lips. "I may be. I'm just telling you how it looks from the outside." He paused, drumming his fingers on the back of my hand. "Do you know what his plans are after he retires?"

"I don't think he even knows yet." I exhaled. "As far as I know, he'll find a new job. Move to a new city. Start a new life. And I..." Lowering my gaze, I sighed. "God, do you really think I'm a placeholder? Something to tide him over between now and when he gets settled into the civilian life?"

"I don't know," Alex said. "I can't read his mind or anything. I'm just telling you what it looks like from where I'm sitting. Which is why I think it would be better for you to talk to him sooner than later, and to be firm in what you are and are not willing to compromise."

175

I nodded. "Yeah, you're probably right."

"And I know you're afraid of his answer when you bring this up," he said, his tone soft. "But if the answer you're afraid of is the one you get, then maybe it's better to get it now instead of six months or a year down the line." He reached across the table and put a hand on my arm. "Because being with someone shouldn't hurt as much as this is obviously hurting you."

I grimaced. "No, it shouldn't."

"But it does, doesn't it?"

"All the way to the bone."

"And is it worth it?"

"Not the way it is right now, no. You're right, I can't put myself through this. I know he's not out, and of course I get that, but I can't be his secret or his booty call. And as much as I don't want to think it, I can't make myself believe he really wants more from me than that."

"I'm sorry it didn't turn out the way you'd hoped," Alex said softly.

"Yeah. Me too."

We finished our coffee, and the waitress brought the check by. Alex reached for it, but I grabbed it first.

"It's on me." Grinning halfheartedly, I added, "I'm assuming the impromptu therapy session will just go on my next bill?"

Alex laughed. "I can't bill anyone until I actually graduate, so I guess you're off the hook."

"Well, thank God for that."

After I'd paid, we left the café, and Alex drove me back to my condo. He put the car in park and let the engine idle. "So, you going to talk to him?"

"Yeah. I'll, um..." I waved a hand. "Wait until it's not quite so late at night, but yeah, I'll talk to him."

Alex smiled. "Good luck."

"Thanks." I leaned across the console and hugged him and then got out of the car.

I walked into my condo on numb, heavy legs. I went through the motions of my evening routine, minus the glass of wine or the hour on the webcam with Adam, and gradually made my way into the bedroom.

All the while, my mind replayed the conversations I'd had with Kieran and Alex, and the conversation I needed to have with Adam.

The guys were right, of course. I needed to talk to Adam, and I was scared to death to talk to Adam.

Ideally, I'd do it when I saw him next, but that wouldn't be fair to him. He'd worked his ass off for twenty years to earn this retirement, and I wouldn't tarnish that for him. But after that weekend, we'd talk. We had to. Otherwise I'd find reason after reason to put it off.

Mostly because I was scared I knew what the answer would be. And, truth be told, even if he wasn't just keeping me around as a convenient—sort of—piece of ass while his life was in flux, I needed to cut my losses and move on. Like Alex had said, I couldn't be a doormat. There were things I wanted and needed, and one thing I didn't want or need was to be someone's second choice. Now that Alex had mentioned it, I couldn't help thinking Adam had come back to me now because I was no longer in competition with the career and the marriage that meant so much to him.

The fallback. The spare. The sure thing when he was done doing everything—everyone—else on his bucket list.

Or, worse, the placeholder to tide him over until someone better came along.

I dropped onto the end of my bed and cradled my face in both hands. I didn't cry. I didn't really hurt, which surprised me. I was mostly numb. I felt empty, hollow, and at the same time like a huge ball of lead had set up shop in the pit of my stomach.

If we could get this relationship off the ground, I knew damn well I'd go through hell and back to save it if anything ever threatened it. But that was a two-way street. I needed to know Adam would do the same, and he hadn't even stuck around to keep our friendship going in the past.

I loved him. I always would.

But more and more, I realized moving on was the right thing. This would be the best thing for me, and for us.

I hoped.

Chapter Fifteen

In spite of his invitation and my promise to fulfill it, I almost didn't go to Adam's retirement. The lines needed to be redrawn, and then I needed some space. Some time. At the very least, a conversation to lay down those lines, and then some breathing room to let it all sink in.

But I'd promised him I'd be here, and this ceremony meant a lot to him, so I kept my mouth shut. Let him have his moment. He'd been working toward this for twenty years, and I wouldn't taint it for him.

So when he pulled into the hotel parking lot the morning of his retirement, I was waiting for him. We hadn't seen each other last night; he'd been tied up with family being in town, and apparently casual booty calls were not on the guest list for dinner with his mother. And anyway, my flight had gotten in late.

But he was here now, and oh my Lord, he looked good. I'd seen photos of him in his khaki uniform, which was hot, but this? It was more like a suit than most of the uniforms I'd seen. Navy blue jacket and tie, with medals on the chest and gold stripes on the sleeves. The hat—the cover, apparently it was called—looked like something I'd seen officers wearing in the movies. White on top, shining black brim. All of that would make any man look incredibly fuckable, but Adam... Jesus.

Are you sure you want to even think about calling it quits?

Yes. Yes, I need to.

I need more than friends with benefits.

We made small talk in the car. Nothing profound or enough to convince me I should change my made-up mind, but enough to keep the silence at bay. When we reached the base, he showed his ID and my driver's license to the sentry, who then waved us through.

The facility where the retirement was being held was typical military: drab, utilitarian exterior, with the interior halls lined with portraits of decorated officers and photos from past wars. In the back, a room resembling a small gymnasium had a podium, a dozen or so rows of chairs and a red carpet between the rows.

As we walked in, Adam's mother, who'd arrived already with his two brothers, turned around.

"Dale," she said with the phoniest smile *ever*. "What an unexpected surprise!" Her gaze slid toward her son, then back to me, and the fake smile brightened to an even less believable degree. She'd never liked me, and obviously twenty years hadn't done a damned thing to temper that. I'd forgotten just how much I'd horrified his parents back when they'd suspected I was *like that* and were certain I was going to turn their military-bound athlete son into a cock-smoking queer. Her contempt was just as strong now as it ever was. Probably because she *knew* now that I was the goddamned flaming fag they always whispered I was. Homophobic bitch.

"Mrs. O'Connor," I said with equally fake enthusiasm. "It's so nice to see you."

"Oh yes," she said through her teeth. "*Lovely* to see you."

Adam's eyes darted back and forth between us, and he gulped. "Well. Um. Mom, you and the family can sit up front. Dale, you..." He glanced at his mom, then looked at me. "Do you..."

I gestured at one of the rows on the opposite side. "I can sit over there. It's fine."

"Okay. Okay, that works." He did a piss-poor job of hiding the relief in his expression, but I kept myself from rolling my eyes. Pushing forty and still couldn't let Mom suspect he was gay. Poor bastard. Maybe he'd tell her when he found a boyfriend worth taking home.

I started to go so I could take my seat, but Adam stopped me.

He leaned in and lowered his voice. "Get a center-aisle seat if you can. Otherwise good luck getting out when this is all over."

"Duly noted," I said with a nod. As he suggested, I took a seat on the center aisle end of one of the middle rows. I didn't mind sitting away from his family. In fact, I was happy to do it. I wasn't part of the family, after all, and spending any more time around his mother's cold shoulder was going to leave me with a serious case of hypothermia. Sitting over here, surrounded by hot uniformed men, was absolutely the better alternative.

As if on cue, Mrs. O'Connor looked over her shoulder and offered another one of those tight-lipped smiles that made me want to fuck with her.

Keep it up, bitch, and I'll tell you in great detail what your son's cock tastes like.

I ignored her as best I could, though, and paid attention to the ceremony as it began. I'd never been to a military function like this before, but I'd heard about them. Long speeches. Pomp and circumstance. The military was all about tradition and ceremony, and they didn't take retirements lightly.

The chaplain gave a convocation. The guys who worked for Adam presented him with a plaque. The other chiefs gave him one as well. The commanding officer gave a long-drawn-out speech. More plaques, a medal, more speeches.

I didn't hear a lot of it, though. I was too focused on Adam. On the lump that had taken up what seemed to be permanent residence in my throat. Seeing him one last time, spending one last weekend together to close the book on anything beyond friendship, had looked like a good idea on paper, but too late I realized it wasn't. I should have bowed out of this weekend and just ended things over the phone. Not my preferred means of breaking it off with someone, but a necessity in a long-distance relationship.

Relationship? Was that what this was? Please. It was sex. A hat tip to the friendship we'd had way back when, but mostly just sex.

Except for those staggeringly romantic moments. The long kiss in the rain. Fucking in ways that could only be construed as making love. The fact that I'd refused to ever have unprotected sex with any man, and then turned around and *wanted* it with him. This wouldn't be easy because it wasn't nearly as simple as I'd convinced myself it was, and coming here to California this time was a huge mistake. This wound didn't need any more salt.

Maybe we weren't even cut out to be friends anymore. Too many lines had been crossed, and I couldn't look at him now without that ache swelling deep in my chest. I didn't want to cut him out of my life, but he didn't want what I did, and somewhere along the line, self-preservation had to come into play.

My eyes started stinging, so I tore my gaze away from him and made myself concentrate on the other men in the room. That wasn't actually too difficult. All these hot young men in uniform? Be still, my beating heart. And hardening cock. And...yeah, everything.

I used to annoy the hell out of Ethan because he wasn't a fan of flaming queens like me, but what he didn't understand was how easy it was for me to scope out potential fucks in a crowd. Nothing screamed *"Come flirt with me, darling, I definitely bat for your team!"* like a guy like me. Which meant the guys who were normally afraid of a potential ass-kicking had no trouble approaching me, since there was precisely zero risk of me being straight. As a result, it wasn't hard to home in on even the subtly gay men. They were the ones who didn't mind making eye contact.

And if they held that eye contact? *Message received, lad. I'll be with you shortly.*

Maybe. Hot and willing were fine and good, but it remained to be seen if I'd actually be in the mood any time soon.

"And now," one of the speakers said. "Chief O'Connor gets to say a few words before we wrap this thing up. Chief?"

Everyone applauded and some of the men cheered as Adam approached the podium. His speech was a relatively brief one, mostly giving nods to people who'd mentored him and to some of his sailors.

Then he paused. It was a long pause. A loaded one, if I knew him. His expression became one of intense concentration, his eyes focused on something on the podium. Maybe his speech wasn't over yet after all.

He squared his shoulders. Took a deep breath. Lifted his gaze. Then he picked up the cards from which he'd been reading his speech and folded them in half. Silently, he slipped them into his inside jacket pocket before he rested a hand on the side of the podium.

"So this is the part where my little speech is going to go off the rails, and you'll all have to forgive me if I ramble a bit. I need to say some things and they're just..." He paused, shaking his head. "They're just not the kinds of things I can write down and rehearse, so I'm going to improvise."

He glanced at me. Then he looked down at the podium and took another breath. As he lifted his gaze again, he said, "There's always been an impression that chief petty officers lead in a 'do as I say, not as I do' style."

A few people laughed quietly, and a faint smile appeared on Adam's lips for a fleeting second.

"I hope," he went on, "that I've not led in that manner. And if I have, then I hope the hard-earned wisdom I'm about to offer will make up for that, and that some of you here might learn from my mistakes. That maybe some of you will do as I say, and not as I stupidly did." He paused again and swallowed hard. "I've had a fantastic career. I'd like to think I've done good things for my country and for the sailors who led me and who I've led."

The crowd erupted with cheers and applause, and a moment later, everyone stood. Adam's cheeks lit up, and he smiled, but then he gestured for everyone to sit back down.

Once the room was again quiet, he continued. "I've had a fantastic career, but twenty years is a long time. A very long time. And after two decades, more than half of my life and all of my adult life, it's painful to look back and realize some of the things I gave up. Of course the military life is all about sacrifice, but sometimes those sacrifices are greater in hindsight. And some of them, perhaps, were not sacrifices that ought to have been made."

I blinked. He'd never been the particularly sentimental type and struggled when it came to expressing emotions. This was...so not like him.

Adam cleared his throat. "I especially realize than when I look back and see that I may have, in the name of keeping this career afloat, hurt people along the way. And if there is anything I regret over the last twenty years, it's that I chose the easy path. I chose to follow my career and leave people behind when I could have made it work."

He shifted his weight and fell silent for a moment, maybe to collect himself, or maybe just to let the words sink in for a moment. Finally, he said, "If I can offer one piece of advice to you junior sailors, those of you in your first or second enlistments who haven't yet invested so many years in the navy, it's to remember that the people you love are the reason you're in the navy. You're fighting for their freedom and for their way of life. So you fight, and you work, and you also make damn sure that in five, ten and fifteen years, when you're standing up here like I am now, getting ready to retire, those people are here with you too."

Some of the guys exchanged puzzled glances. Adam's mother furrowed her brow, her lips pulled into a thin, taut line.

Adam didn't look at her. "There were rules in place when I enlisted. In fact, those rules were still in place even when some of you younger sailors enlisted. And those rules required me to choose between the navy and someone I loved."

Puzzled glances became muffled whispers, as if people were putting two and two together.

"And even without those rules in place," Adam said, "that choice will still be something some of you or your fellow sailors may feel you have to make. And I just hope that if you are called upon to make that choice, between the navy and someone you love, that you make the right choice. Because it's only now, twenty years too late"—Adam looked *right* at me— "that I realize I made the wrong one."

My heart was in my throat. I held my breath.

Adam went on. "They say if you love something, let it go, and if it comes back, it's yours. But sometimes letting go is a mistake. And sometimes what you love comes back, and comes back again, and then finally gives up and stops coming back before you realize what you had." He paused. "And in the end, that's how you lose the love of your life."

My heart stopped. My throat was so tight, air wouldn't move through it, but I couldn't breathe anyway.

Adam, however, wasn't finished yet, and he took a deep breath. "So I want to take this opportunity to thank that person, that love of my life, for coming back. I know things have never been easy where we were concerned, and I can't imagine I've ever been an easy person to love, but..." He paused, exhaling heavily, and then pulled in another deep breath. "But Dale, if you'll have me, I won't let you go this time."

My jaw fell open.

People whispered behind their hands and looked around, expressions ranging from confused to downright stunned.

My heart lurched back into motion as Adam left the podium and came down the steps. He came right up to me and extended his hand.

Shocked whispers rippled through the gathered crowd, and I realized most of them must have thought Dale was a female name.

With his outstretched hand, he beckoned, and he smiled.

My heart thundered. My stomach fluttered. I'd come all this way to see him this one last time, ready to call it off and say *let's be friends* and was ready to move on, and now...this?

I reached for his hand, my own shaking. His was damp with sweat as he closed it around mine, and I stood in spite of my trembling knees. We were eye to eye now, facing each other in the middle of a sea of murmuring men, and I held my breath, wondering what the hell happened next.

Adam let go of my hand and reached for my face. "I know I've screwed this up before," he said softly. "But will you give me a chance to get it right this time?"

I couldn't speak, so I just nodded.

And right there, in front of his family, his shipmates and his friends, Adam cupped my face in both hands and kissed me.

"I love you," he whispered.

"I love you too."

"I'm sorry it took so long for me to do this."

I sniffed sharply and smiled. "You were worth the wait."

He returned the smile and then let me go. As I sank back into my chair, he returned to the podium to finish his speech. I was keenly aware of all the eyes on me and all the "Did that really happen?" whispering going on, but I didn't look anywhere except right at Adam.

"Well," he said, pausing to clear his throat. "I'm pretty sure that wasn't how you all expected this retirement to go, but...there it is. And yes, in case anyone hadn't put two and two together, I'm gay."

There was a moment of tense, uncomfortable silence.

And then everyone broke into applause. A few stayed frozen—Adam's mother, some of the older guys, a handful of the younger ones—but the majority of the audience applauded. Loudly. One guy stood up. Then two. Then an entire row. If I could have moved, or trusted my knees to stay under me, I would have done the same, but I was still just trying to steady myself after that shock.

Someone clapped my shoulder. Another turned around and shook hands with me. He spoke—congratulating me, maybe?—but my heart was beating so fast and hard, I had no idea what he said.

In the front row, Adam's mother wasn't standing, but she did clap, though her taut lips said as much as her refusal to stand. That was going to be an uncomfortable mother-son discussion after all this was over.

The applause calmed, the crowd sat back down, and Adam finished his speech. There were a few traditional rituals at the end—Adam being symbolically relieved of his watch, mostly—and then the ceremony adjourned. More handshakes and congratulations to Adam, a few smiles and disgusted looks directed at me, and the crowd slowly dissipated as people headed back to work.

Adam's mother came out of the cluster of people and regarded me with a steely expression. "Well. I guess that explains why you flew so far to see him retire."

I smiled as sweetly as I could. "I wouldn't have missed it."

If the woman's lips got any thinner...

Adam appeared beside us.

"That was a lovely speech," his mother said, very nearly growling but still managing to stay polite. "Obviously your men thought so."

"Thanks," Adam said through gritted teeth. He glanced at me, eyebrows raised apologetically.

"I thought it was a nice speech," I said and smiled again. No way was that woman putting a damper on this.

His mother huffed like she always did when she was irritated. "Well, I'm sure you'll understand if everyone needs a little time to"—her eyes slid toward me, then back toward Adam—"adjust."

Adam put his arm around my waist. "Take all the time you need."

After a few icy looks, the family left the room.

And suddenly, we were alone. There were a few guys left picking up chairs and cleaning up from the ceremony, but nearly everyone was gone. As far as I was concerned, we were the only two men left in the world right then.

Adam turned to me. "I wasn't going to say all that. Not publicly. But I've been thinking about us a lot lately, and about the future, and I just, I couldn't—"

"Adam." I touched a finger to his lips. "You don't have to explain yourself."

"No, I do. Walking away from you has always been the biggest mistake of my life." He gently pulled my hand away and then kissed my forehead. "I love you, Dale."

And you'll never know how close I came to making the very same one.

But I just whispered, "I love you too."

And as the words rolled off my lips and Adam pulled me into a gentle kiss, the weight of twenty long, long years finally slipped off my shoulders.

Chapter Sixteen

We didn't say much on the way back to the hotel. We didn't say anything at all on the way from the car to my room. I closed the door behind us, and we faced each other.

When I couldn't take the silence anymore, I pulled in a breath. "Everything you said up there. It was…"

"I meant every word." He stepped toward me. "I'm just sorry it took me so long to figure it all out."

I leaned against the door, torn between staying right there and crossing the floor to reach for him. I wanted him, I wanted to have him in my arms, but something felt…unfinished.

Adam moistened his lips. "What's wrong?"

I avoided his eyes. "I'm just… I guess I was having second thoughts about us before I came down here. And after everything you said, I want to believe I was wrong, but…"

"What were you worried about?"

I took a breath. "The thing is, when we're in bed, I feel like I'm your lover. Every time we've been together, it's been like that. But as soon as the lights come on and we're outside the bedroom, I don't feel like anything more than your friend."

"That's just it, Dale," he whispered, reaching for me. "You *are* my friend. You're my best friend. That's why I'm in love with you. I meant everything I said up there." He touched my face. "Leaving you behind is the biggest regret I've ever had. I missed out on twenty years that could have been spent with you." He lifted my chin so we were looking in each other's eyes. "I don't want to miss out on the next twenty."

"I want to believe that," I said. "God, Adam, I do. I just know how much it hurt the last couple of times, and I'm not sure I can go through that a third time."

"You won't. Not this time."

Holding his gaze, I swallowed hard. "If we do this, it won't be easy. We still live hundreds of miles apart."

"I know. We'll work on that." He kissed me gently. "We have tonight together. Then we'll just take it a day at a time."

"Flying back and forth could get expensive."

He shrugged. "It'll be worth it. I always swore up and down I wouldn't do the long-distance thing. But with you, my God, it's so worth it."

I chewed my lip. Damn, but I wanted to believe him.

He leaned in and kissed me again. "Do, um, do you remember when I told you I'd never been with another man?"

I nodded.

"There was a little more to that."

I lifted my eyebrows. "Was there?"

Adam nodded. "Truth was, I was always afraid for my career, so I didn't put a lot of effort into finding guys, even though I did want to." He stroked my hair. "I've been attracted to other men, but that first night we had together, that's the only time in my life I had the chance to be with a man while I wasn't technically in the military. And every time I've thought about being with another man since then, I've had to weigh it with the consequences to my career." He cupped my face in his hands. "Dale, you're the only one I've ever wanted bad enough to ignore those consequences."

My breath caught. "I...really?"

"Yeah." He caressed my cheek. "That was when I knew I'd screwed up when I left you behind. When I realized I was willing to get caught with you, even if it meant my career was fucked."

"I'd never ask you to risk a career for me, Adam."

"I know." He kissed my forehead. "But I would. That's the thing." He drew back, looking in my eyes. "This whole thing scares me to death, and I don't know where it'll go, but more and more"—he stroked my face with the backs of his fingers—"I've realized I would do anything for you." Leaning in closer, he whispered, "And anything to keep from losing you."

Oh. God. Adam. My heart.

"You won't lose me." I cupped his face in both hands. "I'm not going anywhere."

"Neither am I," he said and kissed me.

My whole body relaxed against his. I believed him. For all my fears and for all I'd convinced myself it wasn't really me he wanted, I believed him now.

I believed him. I loved him. And I wanted him.

I pulled him closer and kissed him harder. He pushed me up against the door, and I pressed my hardening erection against his so he knew in no uncertain terms that I was as turned on and desperate as he was.

"Bed," he murmured between kisses.

"Yes."

He pulled me toward him, off the door, and we left a trail of shoes across the room to the bed. Adam pushed my shirt up and off. His medals clanked as his jacket hit the floor. With every piece of his uniform, we stripped away the military, the navy that had been one of the reasons we'd been apart for so long. It was gone. It no longer had a hold on him and couldn't keep him away from me anymore.

The way he touched me and kissed me, *nothing* was keeping him away from me anymore. He gave as good as he got, shoving clothes out of the way and kissing, tasting, biting exposed flesh. He pulled me down on top of him, and though there was nothing graceful or dignified about how we struggled our way out of all these goddamned clothes, I didn't care, because his body was hot and hard and, finally, naked.

"L-lube." He licked his lips. "Do you have any?"

"Of course I do." *And you don't need to know how close I came to leaving it at home this time.* I leaned over the edge of the bed and found the small bottle in my bag.

He took it from me and poured some into his hand. I shivered, anticipating having him fuck me, but instead, he reached for me. The twin shock of cool lube and warm skin made me suck in a breath, and I closed my eyes as he stroked my cock with a slick, tight fist. "I want you to fuck me," he breathed. "Ever since the first time, I can't... I... God, I want you like that again."

"Oh my God..."

"Will you?"

"Yes." I blinked my eyes into focus. "Turn around."

He released me and did as I asked. Foreplay? Oh, fuck foreplay. Every time I'd had him, I'd needed him right now, foreplay be damned, and tonight was no exception. My heart was going a mile a minute as I knelt behind him. Just the simple act of putting some lube on him and teasing him with my fingers to relax him had me lightheaded and ready to come.

Not yet. Please, not yet.

Steadying him with a hand on his hip, I guided myself to him.

"Dale..." He leaned back against me, pressing against the head of my cock. "Please..."

I pressed harder. My vision blurred as my cock slid into him. With each stroke, I gave him more, and with each stroke, I fell apart a little more. We'd made it. We were here. All the pretenses of being something else were gone, and finally, we were making love like we meant it.

And my God, I meant it. I leaned down, wrapped my arm around him and buried my face against his neck, breathing him in as I rode him with long, smooth strokes. I didn't care how fast or how hard I fucked him or how long this lasted or how fast we both came, just that I was inside him and against him, and we were moving, and it was incredible.

Then Adam arched his back off my chest. He groaned, shuddering, and as he tightened around my cock, I released a strangled, "Oh God..."

"Oh fuck," he whimpered.

I didn't even try to hold back. Head spinning and heart thundering, I thrust as hard as I could and shuddered as I came inside him.

I pulled out, and my arms and legs refused to hold me up for another instant, so I dropped onto the bed beside him. Adam rolled onto his back, panting and shaking.

"That was..." He paused, wiping sweat from his brow. "Jesus, Dale."

I laughed breathlessly. "You sound surprised."

He eyed me, then chuckled as he slipped his hand into mine. "I guess we should probably clean ourselves up."

"Yeah. We should. Just...gimme a minute."

The hotel room's shower wasn't huge, but for two men wrapped up in a kiss and each other's arms, it was fine. Warm water ran over both of us as we lazily made out in between our half-assed efforts to get clean.

Eventually, we got out and dried off, and then left the small bathroom.

Adam pulled back the sheets and gestured for me get in first. He joined me, and we pulled the covers up over us. He wrapped his arms around me. I rested my head on his shoulder. We fit together so perfectly. When we were fucking, when we were just cuddled up like this, it was perfect.

After a while, I said, "There is one thing I have to ask about your speech today."

He tensed a little. "Oh yeah?"

I propped myself up and looked him in the eyes. "Did you *really* just come out to your mother like that?"

Laughing softly, he shook his head. "I told her last night. Honestly, after that conversation, I'm surprised she showed up today at all." He grimaced. "She was *not* happy. But I wanted her to have some warning."

"So, aside from now, and from talking to her last night, you've been in the closet all this time?"

He nodded. "I didn't have much choice."

"That must have been hell."

"Honestly?" He ran his fingers through my hair. "I never met anyone who made me want to open up that part of my life to everyone else. It wasn't hell until you came back." Caressing my cheek, he said, "That was when I realized how much I wanted to be with you. When hiding who I was meant hiding you."

"But...what if I'd said no?" I said. "You put yourself out there, in front of everyone, I..."

"That wouldn't have changed how I felt. If you walked away, then I'd have let you go, but I wanted you—and everyone else in that room—to know I'm in love with you."

I exhaled hard but didn't speak.

"You didn't say yes because of the audience, did you?" he asked.

"Of course not. I feel this way about you either way, but I'll admit..."

He smoothed my hair. "You're still worried about this."

"I'd be lying if I said I wasn't." I trailed my fingertips along the edge of his jaw. "I believe you. I believe everything you said up there. I'm just..."

"Scared?"

I nodded.

"So am I." He closed his hand around mine and brought it up so he could kiss the backs of my fingers. "This scares the hell out of me."

"It does?"

Adam nodded. "I know how I feel about you, which is why I'm terrified of losing you again. I mean, you were the reason I..." Trailing off, he kept his eyes down.

I touched his hand. "Adam?"

He was quiet for a long moment, but finally spoke. "Career aside, you were the reason I was never with another man."

"What do you mean?"

He swallowed. "I was attracted to other men, and I certainly felt some chemistry with a few, and I didn't want to risk my career, but the other problem was I kept..." He chewed his lip. "I kept comparing them to you."

"For twenty years?"

Adam nodded. Then he reached for my hand. "I know I'm asking a lot of you right now. But I want to make the effort and see where this goes this time. I just... I guess I need *you* to meet *me* halfway."

I shifted. "How so?"

"I'm not very good at being open about these things. Was one of the things my second wife hated about me. But I want to be. And I want to be with you. Can you be patient with me and keep an open mind? That's all I ask."

I held his gaze. "You know it hurt like hell the last two times, right?"

He nodded. "Yes. I do, and I'm sorry. And I understand that you want to protect yourself. I would too." He squeezed my hand. "Look, I know I did you wrong in the past. I want to fix that. I don't know if we can make something work, or if we're too different now after all this time." He touched my face. "But will you...will you meet me in the middle? Give me a chance to be what you've deserved from the beginning?"

"Adam." I stroked his hair. "I don't care what I deserve. You're everything I *want*." Looking him in the eyes, I whispered, "I love you."

"I love you too," he said and wrapped his arms around me. "More than I can possibly tell you."

I screwed my eyes shut and buried my face against his neck, so relieved that after all this time, after all the stumbling and wrong turns, we were here. We'd made it to this. The future was as uncertain as any future ever was, perhaps more so, but we'd made it this far.

Maybe I was setting myself up to get hurt. Maybe I was on a collision course with a hell of a heartache and a pile of frequent-flier miles. Where we ended up, only time would tell.

But it meant the chance to have what I was sure, deep down, this could be.

And I would gladly take that risk.

Epilogue

A few months later

"This is like déjà vu all over again." Rhett tugged at his bowtie. "Except I won't be quite so front and center this time."

"Yeah, not *this* time." Ethan looked up from adjusting his cufflink. "You're not getting stage fright or anything, are you?"

"Me? Of course not."

As one, all three of us looked at Kieran. He blinked. "What?"

"How about you?" I asked with a grin. "Getting any stage fright?"

"Nerves?" Rhett asked.

"Panic attacks?" Ethan chimed in.

Kieran rolled his eyes. "Fuck you guys. I'm fine."

"I'll say you are," Ethan said with a grin, making no small gesture of looking Kieran up and down.

"Dirty bastard," Kieran muttered, and they both laughed.

The door opened, and my heart fluttered as Adam came in. He and I weren't in tuxes since we weren't part of the wedding party like Rhett and Ethan, but damn, he looked good in a coat and tie.

He slipped an arm around my waist. "Everyone just about ready? The minister's making some noise about wanting to get started."

"We're getting there," Ethan said.

"Man, it is just one wedding after another around here," Kieran said. "So who's up next? I mean, Tyson and Sabrina are next month, but who's after that?" He looked at me, and his eyebrows rose.

I patted Adam's arm. "Oh, you know. We don't need to hurry these things."

"Hurry them?" Ethan blinked. "It isn't like you guys just met last week."

"No, that's true." Adam drew me closer and kissed my cheek. "But we'll get there."

My heart fluttered. I bit back a stunned, "*We will?*" Instead, I cleared my throat and said, "Sabrina and Tyson have been engaged long enough, anyway. It really wouldn't be polite for us to get married before them."

"Exactly," Adam said. "Ladies first."

"Oh God," Ethan said. "I'm not sure I'm ready for that."

"What?" I laughed. "Why not?"

"It hasn't even been two years since I got married myself," he said. "I'm so not ready for this whole father-of-the-bride thing."

I snickered. "Well, brace yourself, then."

He eyed me. "What's that supposed to mean?"

"She's getting married, sweetheart." I grinned. "You know what the next step after marriage is."

He furrowed his brow. "The next step? What do—" Ethan paled. "Oh dear God."

"Relax." Rhett squeezed Ethan's shoulders but couldn't help snickering, which drew a dirty look from his husband.

"Look on the bright side, Ethan," I said. "People will have a reason to say you look young."

Ethan arched an eyebrow. "How so?"

I smirked. "You do look young for a grandfather."

"Oh fuck *you*."

Kieran laughed. Then he closed his eyes and took a long, deep breath. As he slowly let it out, I asked, "You sure you're okay?"

He nodded. "Yeah. Just some nerves." He looked at me. "Would you mind checking on Alex? Knowing him, he's probably a nervous wreck."

"Sure." I turned to Adam. "I'll be right back."

"Okay," he said with a smile and kissed me lightly.

I left the room and headed down the hall in search of one of the nervous grooms. My stomach was fluttering like I was in Alex's or Kieran's shoes, and my mind kept going back to that comment Adam had made when Kieran asked if we were getting married anytime soon.

"We'll get there."

Oh, really, Adam?

It wasn't like we were just casually dating or anything. Adam had moved up to Seattle and into my condo a few months ago. The job market still sucked, and he was still struggling to find something, but his retirement from the navy kept him afloat. Especially now that we were splitting bills and living expenses.

Up until today, though, neither of us had really broached the subject of getting married. Not even in an offhand, in-passing kind of way. Adam sure as hell didn't mention it, and I'd never pushed because I didn't imagine it was something he wanted after three divorces.

"We'll get there."

Was that just a way of politely redirecting the conversation? Or what?

Stop reading so much into it.

I shook my head and continued outside in search of Alex.

I found him out by the garden beside the church with Sabrina, Tyson and one other guy. It didn't take a genius to figure out who the third guy was. He was a little taller than Alex, and his hair was a bit longer—not to mention completely dark instead of painstakingly highlighted—but the family resemblance was definitely there.

As I approached, Sabrina turned, and she grinned. "Hey, you!"

I held out my arms to hug her. "Good to see you, darling. And you look fabulous."

"Thank you," she said and hugged me.

I shook hands with Alex and Tyson, and then Alex said, "Have you met my brother yet?"

"No, I haven't had the pleasure." I extended my hand. "Dale Ramsey."

"Lee Corbin." He smiled as he shook my hand, and my God, they were definitely brothers. "Nice to meet you."

"You too." To Alex, I said, "Well, you look amazing, as always. How are you feeling? Nervous yet?"

He smiled and shrugged. "Not really. What about Kieran?"

"A little jittery. I think he'll be all right, though."

"He'd better be." Lee pulled back his tuxedo sleeve and checked his watch. "We're five minutes from show time."

"Five minutes." Alex took a deep breath, probably unaware how much he was mirroring his nervous husband-to-be. "Okay. I think I'm ready for this."

"You'll be fine," Lee said. "Just don't lock your knees, and remember to breathe."

"Remember to breathe." Alex rolled his shoulders. "Right. Got it." He eyed his brother. "If I pass out, you'd better catch me. That's the best man's job, you know."

Lee laughed and clapped Alex's shoulder. "You might want to just stay on your feet."

"Jerk," Alex muttered, but they looked at each other and laughed, and then we all headed inside.

The ceremony was beautiful. What wedding wasn't? And the reception was small but lovely. During dinner, Alex's brother and Ethan both gave toasts. Of course, just like when he'd read his vows to Rhett at their wedding, Ethan managed to move almost everyone in attendance to tears. The son of a bitch would probably have us all *bawling* when Sabrina got married next month.

As the reception went on, the room was getting a little stuffy, so Adam and I wandered outside.

Out on the patio, I leaned against the railing, champagne flute between my fingers. "So, um..."

Adam looked at me. "Hmm?"

I cleared my throat. "Did you mean what you said earlier? That we'd...get there?"

"Do you think we won't?"

"I don't know. We've never really talked about it. I didn't know if it was something you wanted to do again." I paused, cringing. "I mean, if you—"

"I know what you meant." He sipped his champagne and then shrugged as he looked out at the reception hall's garden. "I've tried the whole marriage thing three times and failed. But I'm not opposed to it."

"But are you..." I hesitated. "Is it something you *want*?"

He set his glass on the railing. Then he took mine and did the same. Hands free, he wrapped his arms around me. "There isn't a thing I would change about us, Dale. I love you. I love our life together." He reached up and brushed a few strands of hair out of my face. "No, I'm not opposed to us getting married."

"But...?"

His eyes lost focus. "I..."

I quirked an eyebrow at him. "Is this the part where you tell me you don't see why we should get married?"

"No, not at all." He laughed softly, his cheeks coloring. "I guess it's just hard to put into words." He chewed his lip. "Look, I've been down the aisle and through divorce proceedings enough times to be a little jaded. I won't deny that. After that sort of thing, it's hard not to see marriage as more than a piece of paper. A formality. And I do want that formality for us. Don't get me wrong. Yes, I do want us to get married."

My heart jumped, but something in his voice kept me from relaxing just yet. "You want us to get married, but...?"

"I'm not very eloquent with this stuff. I'm sorry." He sighed. "Look, I went into marriage like it was just another step. I didn't take it as seriously as I really should have. My ex-wives? They treated getting married like a way of sealing the deal. 'There's a ring on his finger, so he's not going anywhere.'"

"So like a golden handcuff."

"Kind of. Yeah."

"That's not what I want, just so you know."

"I know." He kissed my forehead. "I've never thought you did. I guess what I'm trying to say," he whispered, drawing back so we made eye contact again, "is that the rings and marriage license won't change *this* for me. What we are." He stroked my cheek with the backs of his fingers. "Not because I don't value marriage, because I do value it the way I didn't before. And it's not that I wouldn't want to marry you. Quite the opposite, believe me. It's just that..." He paused, eyes losing focus.

I squeezed his hand, hoping he took it as reassuring.

Finally, he spoke, and I thought his voice shook a little as he said, "I just need you to know that nothing could ever make me more committed to you than the twenty years I spent without you."

All the breath slipped out of my lungs at once.

"I love you, Dale," he said. "And I would be honored to be your husband."

Words failed me. Completely. I couldn't speak at all.

So I just pulled Adam into my arms and kissed him.

"I love you," I whispered.

He smiled. "I love you too."

"*There* you are," Rhett's voice turned us both around. "We were starting to wonder if you guys had taken off."

"Taken off?" I put a hand to my chest and gasped. "Before the bouquet toss?"

Rhett rolled his eyes.

Adam snickered as he slid an arm around my waist. "We were just getting some air."

"Uh-huh." Rhett arched an eyebrow. "Sure you—"

"No wonder you came looking for us," I said. "You were hoping to join in."

Sighing with exasperation, Rhett shook his head. "Yes, Dale. That's it." He gestured toward the reception hall. "Kieran wants to round us all up for some group pictures. You guys in?"

"Sure, yeah." I smiled. "We'll be right there."

Rhett nodded. "Great. Now I just need to chase down the damned photographer."

He headed back. Adam and I exchanged glances, then followed Rhett back inside. Slipping my hand into his elbow, I looked up at him again and smiled. He returned it and rested his hand over the top of mine.

It had taken us twenty years to meander back into each other's arms. I could wait a little longer for the ring.

Yeah, I would wait for the ring.

Because right now, I had everything I could ever ask for.

About the Author

L.A. Witt is an abnormal M/M romance writer currently living in the glamorous and ultra-futuristic metropolis of Omaha, Nebraska, with her husband, two cats, and a disembodied penguin brain that communicates with her telepathically. In addition to writing smut and disturbing the locals, L.A. is said to be working with the US government to perfect a genetic modification that will allow humans to survive indefinitely on Corn Pops and beef jerky. This is all a cover, though, as her primary leisure activity is hunting down her arch nemesis, erotica author Lauren Gallagher, who is also said to be lurking somewhere in Omaha.

Website: http://www.loriawitt.com

Twitter: @GallagherWitt

Blog: http://gallagherwitt.blogspot.com

The virgin isn't the only one with something to lose...

The Closer You Get
© *2011 L.A. Witt*

Self-described manwhore Kieran Frost is loving the single life. Two years after moving to Seattle, he still has his friends with benefits, Rhett and Ethan, plus a never-ending supply of gorgeous, available men wandering through the bar where he works. A relationship? Spare him the drama and heartbreak. He's got no complaints about his unattached lifestyle.

When Rhett's daughter introduces him to newly-out-of-the-closet Alex Corbin, Kieran's interest perks up. After all, the quiet ones are always the freaks in bed. But Alex isn't just shy and reserved. He's a virgin in every sense of the word, having never even kissed anyone else.

Kieran is no one's teacher, and his first instinct is to run like hell in the other direction. But his conscience won't let him throw the naïve kid to the wolves for someone else to take advantage of. The plan is to introduce Alex to his own sexuality, pull him out of his shell, then go their separate ways.

It's the perfect, foolproof plan...assuming no one falls in love.

Warning: This sequel to The Distance Between Us *contains a curious virgin, a shameless slut, a trip to a sex shop, and one stubborn heart. Oh, and a dildo.*

Available now in ebook and print from Samhain Publishing.

It's all about the story...

Romance

HORROR

www.samhainpublishing.com

CPSIA information can be obtained at www.ICGtesting.com
Printed in the USA
BVOW05s1040230914

367977BV00002B/22/P

9 781619 219595